Judge Not

An Ivy Greene Mystery, Book 2

By Susan Byrde

Bible quotations and references
https://www.biblegateway.com

ISBN: 978-1-952661-52-5

Judge not, that ye be not judged.
For with what judgment ye judge, ye shall be
judged: and with what measure ye mete, it shall be
measured to you again.

Matthew 7:1-2
KJV

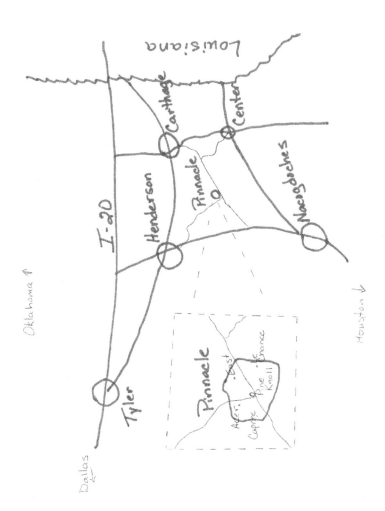

Dear Reader,

If this is your first *Ivy Greene Mystery*, you might need a little background on the setting and characters. Ivy Greene lives in Pinnacle, Texas, with her daughter, Anna Claire, a solid white umbrella cockatoo named Ebony, and two mongrel dogs named Baskin and Robin. Most of Ivy's family lives in Pinnacle, too, including her parents, Karl and Eleanor Gruene (pronounced Green), and her sister, Winter, brother-in-law Henry Kowalski, nieces Mikayla and Meela, and nephew Henry Jr. The only member of the Gruene family not in East Texas is Ivy's brother, Hunter, who lives near Atlanta, Georgia.

At 30(ish), Ivy is a widow. She has her own mobile dog grooming business, so she's out in the community most of the time. There are two men in her life, her teenage crush, James Williamson, is now her next-door neighbor. He is fair-haired with blue-green eyes and a protective-big-brother attitude toward Ivy. The second man is Luke Swaim, Pinnacle's newest police detective. He is tall and dark-haired with striking blue eyes. He earned the nickname The Swami for the simple reason that someone transposed the last two letters of his last name, and it stuck.

As for the community of Pinnacle, it only exists in my mind and on these pages, but if you were to find it in the real world, it would be in the Piney Woods of East Texas - west of the Louisiana border, south of Interstate 20, and north of Nacogdoches. Initially, the area was home to several small towns - Pine Knoll, Nara (named for a Caddo Indian princess) Acer, Capree, LeChance, and East. The civic leaders of these communities decided to gather together, pool their tax-based resources, and save the area from desertion and ruin. They used the first letters of each little burg to form the new city's name. Ivy's hometown was East, and Pine Knoll, the largest of these towns, was home to a private university, Humphrey-Dearing University, that is known for its world-class microbiology research facility, and exceptional pre-med and pre-law curriculums. Incidentally, both of Ivy's parents are employed by the university. Eleanor is the chair of the biology department, and Karl is a semi-retired law professor.

I hope you enjoy this installment of the *Ivy Greene Mysteries.* I'd love to have you join me if you're on Facebook, Instagram, or Twitter. My website, www.susanbyrde.com has links to each of my social media accounts. If you're more of an email fan, feel free to send me a note and let me know what you thought of this story. My email address is susan.byrde@gmail.com.

In the meantime, may the Lord bless you and happy reading!

Sincerely,

Susan Byrde

Chapter 1

Barking.

By itself, the sound of a dog calling out to the world isn't something that makes a person stop and take notice. However, when the neighborhood is typically quiet and the pitch and tone of the dog's voice rapidly changes from "Hey, is anyone out there?" to "Intruder! In MY yard," you pay attention.

I was walking my freshly washed-dried-and-clipped client up his driveway when one of the neighbor dogs began to sound his individual alarm. The newly groomed Roofus, a silver-colored miniature Schnauzer, paused to look around. Roofus and I both cocked our heads—his one way, mine the other—as we tried to identify the source of the vocalizations. I knew most of the dogs in the area, either from my mobile dog-grooming business or my occasional obedience classes, but the sound of this dog didn't ring any familiar bells. Aside from the noise made by the unseen canine, the area was still and quiet. Soon, the other dog fell silent, and my charge performed a tip-to-tail body shake as if to clear the interruption from his mind before he proceeded toward the front door of his home. I glanced up the street to see if anything seemed amiss before accompanying Roofus to the waiting arms of his hu-mom, Cindy.

The closer we got to the porch, the more Roofus' gait changed from a casual stroll to an odd, animated dance. While Cindy waited, her brow arched in curiosity, the dog began a series of moves that belied logic and made him appear to move in all directions at once. With just a few feet remaining between the woman and her fur baby, Cindy clapped her hands and Roofus launched himself into her outstretched arms.

Elsewhere in the neighborhood, the unknown dog began to raise a ruckus again. Throaty warning barks soon became higher pitched and punctuated with an occasional *yip*. Cindy released her happy dog into the house and stepped out onto the front walk with me as we tried to determine whose dog was barking and why.

After a few short moments, the warning barks became more frantic; then there was a prolonged yelp of pain, and . . . silence.

"That was weird," Cindy said.

Still distracted, I nodded as I searched the far end of the block. The dog made no more noises, and even the birds had ceased their symphony. With nothing moving and no other clues as to the wheres or whys of the distressed dog, I finally said, "I'll head that way when I leave and see if I can find out what's going on."

Cindy and I scheduled Roofus' next appointment and parted ways. I climbed back into my van and had just started to secure a few loose items before pulling away when my cockatoo, Ebony, let out a long-and-low wolf whistle. Ebony goes to work with me most days, as he tends to get into trouble when left alone at home for too long. His cage sits behind a divider between the driver's seat and my work area. A rectangular cut-out just above my head allows Ebony to see where we're going and feel connected to me even when I'm driving. An extremely intelligent and vocal bird, Ebony often squawks words from his varied and random repertoire, but rarely whistles. Surprised, and more than a little curious, I glanced up at him and caught the movement of something outside from the corner of my eye—a blur of bright red and green chugging past my van on the sidewalk. Was it a man? He looked to be smiling, his face framed by a torch of red hair. He wore a green shirt, pinkish-white pants, and black socks and shoes. As he drew closer, I realized that not only were his pants missing, but his shirt was glistening, much like the dew shimmers on the early morning grass. Shocked by the spectacle, I continued to stare as his bare backside appeared in my side-view mirror, then disappeared in a dizzying flash of naked flesh.

About the time he cleared my truck, my phone rang. I hit the button on my headset to answer it, fully intending to say something professional like, "Ivy's 'Dos for Dogs, this is Ivy." Instead, I blurted, "I just saw a nekkid man!"

"I'm telling Mama you said the word 'nekkid.'"

My sister Winter said these words in the same sing-song tone I'd heard throughout my childhood. The older sibling, she had spent a lot of time when we were growing up making sure I got away with absolutely nothing. I was sure she was kidding this time, but those three words—"I'm telling Mama"—still sent a shot of adrenaline straight to my heart.

"Then I'm telling her you lied about skipping out on her big dinner last month," I answered.

There was silence on the phone line for a moment. Finally, Winter said, "Fair enough. So, the reason I'm calling is . . ."

As she started rattling off whatever was on her mind, I continued to stare at my side-view mirror. It was now filled with only greenery and sidewalk, but I couldn't shake the odd after-image of a green torso and white fanny disappearing around the bend down the street. *Nekkid man . . . red hair . . . green shirt?* I tried to wrap my mind around it, struggling to find some underlying logic.

Why was the torso of the man green? Had he been wearing a shirt? Had his face seemed too pale? And his smile . . . had it been just a little too enthusiastic? And what about that horrendous red hair?

I shut my eyes to think, muttering "uh-huh" at what I hoped were opportune moments even though I wasn't listening. Suddenly, the reality dawned on me: the man could not have been wearing a shirt because there had been a wide flesh-colored band down the middle of his back. His torso was green because of some sort of body paint, and the stripe had been flesh-colored because it was, well, flesh. It hadn't been green, because when he'd been painting himself, he obviously couldn't reach the middle of his back. The hair jumped out at me because I, too, have red hair, but mine isn't the unnaturally bright red color of the man's. Mine is more ginger—lighter in the summer than in the winter, and naturally curly. The man's hair definitely looked heavily processed. In fact, now that I thought about it, it looked fake. He'd also been wearing a mask—the kind that's made of thin rubber and fits over the top of the head.

With all the images assembled in my brain, I now realized the streaker had been made up to look like, what else? A leprechaun.

I opened my eyes, rolled them high enough so I could almost read my next thought, and groaned. Behind me, Ebony squawked, "Win! Win!" which reminded me that I was supposed to be talking to my sister. Too late. I glanced at the phone and saw the call had been disconnected.

Slightly concerned about what I might have agreed to do – and completely forgetting to check on the barking dog, I cranked up my van, put it in gear, and started for home. It was nearing lunchtime, and I had a sudden craving for Lucky Charms cereal.

Chapter 2

My name is Ivy Greene. You might say humor—
satirical humor—is in my DNA. My parents are two
amazingly intelligent people with common first names,
Karl and Eleanor, and an easy-to-pronounce, yet hard-
to-decipher last name: Gruene (pronounced like the
color green). They willingly admit to planning the
names of their first two children, Hunter and Winter.
When I arrived, I was given the name IndigoViolet.
Mama has always assured everyone that my name was
an accident, that the nurse assigned to name registration
misinterpreted her delirious post-partum mutterings
about the color spectrum—particularly the various
shades of purple—after 48 hours of labor, as my given
name. Considering my mother's track record for
choosing ironic-sounding names, I have always doubted
this story. I don't know what my parents had picked out
for me exactly, but I'm sure it would have followed
along in the same vein. They might have intended to
call me Misty, or Kelly. Of course, now that I think
about it, they could have called me something

genuinely atrocious, like Gan. (Picture this: Mama and Daddy proudly introducing their three children— Hunter, Winter, and Gan Green—phonetically speaking, of course.)

Yikes! Maybe I'd actually gotten off lucky!

Suffice it to say that my life is filled with the comical. Once you get past my given name, IndigoViolet Gruene, and the fact that I married a man whose last name was Greene, you just have to look at the creatures around me to know that I attract wittiness. There's my umbrella cockatoo Ebony—"Ebs" for short— who's covered in snowy-white feathers, including those on his crest that spread out to look like a war bonnet. He and his original owner, Willa Gentry, found me in a park, alone, crying, newly widowed, and just beginning to show my pregnancy. They took me under their proverbial wing and blessed me with a couple of years of unconditional love and support. Willa and her husband, the Colonel, were avid practitioners of irony. Having a solid white bird named Ebony inspired them to adopt a succession of black dogs, which they called Ivory. In total there were four little black dogs of questionable heritage, all named for the creamy color of an elephant's tusk. When Willa passed away, joining her beloved Colonel for some heavenly hijinks, I moved back to my East Texas home with Ebony and my daughter, Anna Claire, and bought a house. We had been in our home just a few short months when two stray dogs took up residence with us. Anna worked on convincing me—by virtue of her beautiful green-brown eyes, puddling with unshed tears—for several days before I said we could keep them, and when I finally caved, she begged me to let her name them. Thus, we now have a scruffy, brown, male terrier mix and a short-legged, black-and-white female Border Collie mix named Baskin and Robin, respectively. We have a handful of chickens, too. I don't think of them as part of the family, but they all have names that change according to Anna's whims.

What can I say? It's in our blood.

A glance at my outside mirror brought to mind the leprechaun again. If he were part of my family, or if it were up to Anna to name him, what would we call him? Nekkid Ned? Leo the Leprechaun? Shamrock Gruene? On second thought, it's probably better that I was the only family member to see him.

Chapter 3

Back out on the main road, I noticed traffic was unusually light. It took me a moment to realize it was the last day before Spring Break for all the local schools. Students from Humphrey-Dearing University had likely skipped or been dismissed from afternoon classes and had hopped into their cars, eager to make the most of their vacation. It was then that the thought of my baby leaving me for almost five days hit me like a frying pan to the forehead. My in-laws were taking Anna Claire on a surprise trip to Disney World. This wouldn't be the first time that we'd be separated for more than a night, but I'd be a bald-faced liar if I said I was looking forward to it.

A quick glance at my watch told me it was twenty minutes before twelve—or ten minutes before Anna's class went to lunch. They were dismissing the kids early today and it occurred to me that two extra hours away—give or take—on the last day before Spring Break wouldn't hurt anyone. Besides, my craving for breakfast foods had intensified, and I wasn't particularly excited about eating by myself.

Yep, that settles it, I thought as I changed lanes and headed for the school to pick up my daughter early.

I managed to get to Pinnacle Christian Academy just as Anna Claire's first grade class was lining up to go to the cafeteria. More than one child looked envious that she was getting to leave early, and based on the general over-activity of the kids, I was reasonably sure her teacher wouldn't be disappointed to have one less wiggly worm to tame after recess.

In a flash, Anna grabbed her backpack and began tugging me down the hallway. She's usually a talkative child, but today she was chattering away with the enthusiasm of an over-caffeinated auctioneer. I caught maybe every third word of her monologue. Fortunately, the only thing required of me was an occasional "Uh-huh" or "Oh, good!"

"And guess what!" she exclaimed as she bounded into my van. "We have homework!"

Since my last response was "Uh-huh," I figured it was time for "Oh, good."

"It is!" The rest of her words faded into the background as I buckled my seatbelt and checked my mirrors for impatient drivers or runaway children.

"Uh-huh," I muttered half-heartedly.

"So, what is it?"

Now I was busted. I hadn't really been listening, and Anna knew it. "What is what?"

"Oh, Mama!" My daughter sighed heavily, and I could virtually hear her shaking her head at me in shame. "Mrs. Danford wants you to tell me your favorite Bible verse and help me learn it. We get to tell them in class on Monday when we get back."

Mrs. Danford was Anna's newest Arts and Religion teacher. The teachers for this subject area rotated throughout the year, which meant the kids had exposure to a different A & R teacher quarterly. I knew this lady had kids of her own, and I couldn't imagine what made her think an assignment over a nine-day break was a good idea. I sighed.

"So, what is your favorite Bible verse?"

There are a lot of people who have spent a great deal of time studying the Bible, but I confess I am not one of those people. I went to church frequently as a child, mostly because I didn't want my daddy to have to go alone. I have actually read the entire Bible, and I read devotional passages every day, but I have yet to pin down one specific passage as my favorite. Still, Anna was waiting for my answer.

"Well, baby, I'll have to think about it." Behind me, Anna groaned. In an effort to assuage her emotional distress, I added, "There are so many things in the Bible I enjoy reading that it's hard to decide on just one."

At least this was close enough to the truth to buy me some time.

Dejectedly, my girl mumbled, "Okay."

I hated that my lack of knowledge had so thoroughly let the air out of her bubble. But I couldn't lie to my baby girl, especially not about the Bible. In hopes of pumping her back up again, I said, "How about we go to Stoney's for lunch?"

She gasped with joy and clapped. "Oh, Mama, can we?"

In his cage, Ebony began to hop up and down while crowing about lunch.

Stoney's is an institution in the Pinnacle

community. Founded more than sixty years ago by a local family, the diner served as *the* daytime meeting place and weekend cruising spot long before any of the fast-food chain restaurants had even thought of staking their claim in our area. A late-night fire had destroyed the original building, but the Stone family had quickly found another location, converting an abandoned grocery store into the current restaurant. To be perfectly honest, I eat at Stoney's almost as often as I eat at home.

We pulled into my favorite parking spot—the one at the end of the building under a huge shade tree—gave Ebony some fresh vegetables, locked up the truck, and went into the diner. The main dining room is enormous, with booths along two walls and the front windows, an open area full of tables in the center, and a traditional chrome soda-fountain-type counter facing the remaining wall. Even with many of the university students away, the diner had plenty of business.

Anna skipped ahead and secured two seats at the nearly empty counter. I slid onto the stool next to her and reached for menus. My child is naturally sensible when it comes to her food, so I expected her to choose a meal from the kids' lunch menu. I can tell you that I'm not really sure where she gets this penchant for healthy food choices, because I'm the type that would happily choose dessert anytime in place of a traditional meal. But in an effort to act a little more like an adult, I began looking at the breakfast offerings, certain it was still early enough to justify a selection from that portion of the menu sweet enough to satisfy my sugar craving.

"Ivy Greene!" My friend Marnie Nichols stood at the far side of the restaurant, shouting my name. Marnie had worked at Stoney's long enough that she, too, was an institution. "I heard you saw a *nekkid* man this morning! Inquiring minds want to know! Who was it?"

The entire lunchtime clientele stopped talking (and probably eating and breathing) and turned to look at me while my face turned fire-engine red. Next to me, Anna gasped, her eyes going as round as saucers. In a scandalized voice, she shouted into the now-silent room, "Mama! Shame on you!"

My head began to throb as my face searched for a color more vibrant than my usual flaming blush.

"Oh, hey there, Anna Claire! I didn't see you come in." Marnie sauntered over to us, mouthing her apology to me as she walked.

Behind me, a handful of people chuckled, and the conversation started up again. Anna continued to stare at me, mouth agape. I prayed for a sinkhole to open up and swallow me. I patted her leg and whispered that she needed to close her mouth, which she did with an audible snap.

Marnie handed us each a placemat to color and a small tin of crayons. She chatted up my daughter while my blood receded to more appropriate locations within my body. Several glances my way told my friend when I was back to normal, and she took our order without further mention of men—nekkid or otherwise.

"Mama's getting the blueberry pancakes. She says you have a magic blueberry tree in the back, so the berries are always fresh." Anna was studying Marnie's expression. "Is that true?"

My friend wiggled her eyebrows at my daughter and whispered conspiratorially, "I'm sworn to secrecy. I can't say."

Anna gasped with delight. "Can I see it?"

"*May* I," I corrected.

"Mama wants to see it, too."

My head still hurt, so I didn't bother correcting her a second time. Marnie flashed a mysterious (and noncommittal) smile at us and sauntered away towards the kitchen.

Anna and I colored while we waited for our food. I was glad that she'd turned her attention to making sure her peacock picture was suitably arrayed with colorful feathers and away from anything having to do with me. Our meal arrived without fanfare—grilled cheese and a side of fruit for my daughter and blueberry pancakes with extra butter for me. When my plate came to rest in front of me, Anna shook her head but didn't comment on my selection.

Eventually, we finished eating. Anna wandered off to look at the gumball machine selections while Marnie cleared our empty dishes.

"I'm sorry about earlier." My friend looked contrite but I saw a glint in her eyes. "Winter came in about fifteen minutes before you and announced it to everyone here. Of course, there weren't as many people in here then."

My only response was a nod.

"So, spill," Marnie said. "Who was it? Was it James or that seriously hot new detective that's been sniffing around you?"

I snorted. James was my next-door neighbor and one of my sister's old boyfriends. I'd had a crush on him for about half my life. The detective *was* nice looking, and we ate lunch together on occasion, but he was hardly "sniffing around" me.

"I've got five bucks riding on The Swami," Marnie prodded.

The Swami was Detective Swaim. In spite of the fact that his name was printed clearly on his departmental ID, and that he frequently corrected people on the pronunciation, most people still called him "The Swami."

"You'd lose," I answered vaguely.

"You mean, you saw James . . ."

"No!" My answer was a little too loud, drawing glances from people nearby. "I was just finishing up a client over on Walnut. Ebony whistled, and I looked up to see a man running by wearing only his shoes. He had a mask on, too, that hid his face. I really couldn't tell you who it was."

"But you could—"

"Mama, can I have a quarter for a gumball?"

Anna's question saved me from any more grilling from Marnie. "It's '*May* I,' Anna, and no. We need to get going."

If I'd had eyes in the back of my head, I'm pretty sure I would have seen both my friend and my daughter rolling theirs at me.

Chapter 4

Anna was about to leave for her trip to Disney with her grandparents—not my parents, mind you, but her paternal grandparents. She knew she was going to see them, and that they had a surprise for her, but she didn't know that she'd be going to *Disney*. I knew the clothes she had were good enough, but that little nagging voice in the back of my mind kept telling me that "good enough" wasn't quite the image I wanted to present to the Greenes.

Enter Small Fries, a kids' boutique with some of the cutest and most reasonably priced clothes *ever*. I'm not a big fan of shopping for myself, but Anna and I both enjoy going to Small Fries.

The store is located in an L-shaped strip mall. There's a Mexican restaurant at one end of the complex and an ice cream parlor at the other. A nail salon has the shop at the bend, and a book store sits between the kids' store and a boutique for teen girls, aptly named "Whatever." There are two challenges when we go shopping at Small Fries: one is trying to avoid the ice cream parlor (which is nearly impossible), and the second is parking. The main lot is small, so spaces are hard to come by, especially for a large vehicle. There's an overflow lot that I use when I'm in my work van, but if you park there, you have to walk right past the restaurant, which exudes enough tantalizing scents of fresh sopapillas and chips to tempt even the most satisfied appetite.

The idea when we entered Small Fries was to pick up a shirt or two, and maybe an extra pair of shorts for Anna's trip. About an hour later, we emerged onto the sidewalk with two Santa-worthy sacks of spring and summer clothing for my daughter and a near-depleted bank balance.

In my defense, they were having a sale.

As we left the store, Anna asked if we could get ice cream. No surprise there. I took a moment—or really, just a split second—to weigh my choices. On the one hand, there was no reason to stop for ice cream *every* time we shopped at Small Fries; on the other, the afternoon had warmed up quite a bit since we'd arrived at the mall. Besides, Anna hadn't complained about trying on clothes (not that she ever did, really), and my stomach felt so empty that I was beginning to wonder if that generous stack of blueberry-laden pancakes had been a figment of my imagination. I caved without bothering to put up a fight. On our way back to my truck, we spotted Detective Luke Swaim exiting the restaurant.

"The Swami" moved to Pinnacle from New Orleans less than a year ago. Tall and lean, with dark hair and deep blue eyes, Luke has a bit of a Cajun accent, one which can be charming and sometimes a little hard to understand. He is strongly built, with an athletic grace, which makes him easy to look at and, on those few occasions where I've been close enough to notice, he smells really good, too. To this point in his Pinnacle Police career, he had managed to charm just about everyone, with the exception of my dad, my neighbor, and my bird.

"Detective Luke!" Anna exclaimed when she saw him. I'm pretty sure she's his number one fan.

"Well, hello, Miss Anna," he replied, meeting us at the corner in front of the nail salon. "What's good at the ice cream shop?"

My daughter held her cone up to him. "I got mint chocolate. It's great. Do you want a bite?"

"No, thank you, Miss Anna. I just finished lunch, and I don't think I have any more room in my stomach." He looked up at me, flashed me a bone-melting smile, and said, "Hello, Ms. Ivy."

I nodded, but before I could speak, Anna piped up again.

"Mama got cherry vanilla ice cream. She *always* gets cherry vanilla."

Swaim nodded. "I think that suits her just fine, Miss Anna."

So, in addition to being good-looking, charming, and having some really nice cologne, Swaim is something of a flirt. He can be serious when he needs to be, but catch him in a casual environment and the southern gentleman in him oozes from his pores. I had yet to succumb, but I often wondered how many of our local ladies swooned when he passed them on the street.

"So, what's going on in the criminal world today, Detective Swaim?" I asked, an involuntary smile gracing my lips before I hid it behind my melting ice cream.

"Funny you should ask," he said. He shifted on his feet, his expression suddenly more serious. "I wanted to talk to you about some animal thefts that have been occurring recently."

This immediately put me on guard. The last time Swaim wanted to talk to me about anything crime-related was last fall when he was investigating a dead body I'd literally tripped over. At that time, I was one of the suspects, and while I had been innocent then—and am now—my adrenaline spiked, and my emotional defenses slipped into place.

"Oh?" This was the best I could do on such short notice. I'm not exactly fast-on-the-draw when it comes to quick replies.

"Yes, ma'am. We've had several reports of pets being taken from yards and homes. Mostly these animals have been large dogs, but there have been a few smaller dogs and a handful of cats. I wanted to ask if you've noticed anything unusual."

"Unusual?" A mostly nekkid leprechaun would definitely fall into the category of unusual, but I didn't see how that related to disappearing dogs.

"Yes, ma'am. Have you noticed any vehicles driving down the street too slow or maybe parked where they shouldn't be?"

As I shook my head no, a random thought rattled around just beyond my grasp. "I haven't noticed anything like that, but to be honest, I'm usually focused on what I'm doing—the walking back and forth, the washing, drying, and clipping needed to finish my job. I hate to admit it, but I don't really look around when I'm working."

Swaim nodded. "That's understandable. What about your bird?"

"What about him?"

"I'm sure I don't have to tell you how valuable that kind of a pet can be. Do you secure him before you leave him alone?"

I had to chuckle at this. Ebony could spend all day basking in admiration, but he isn't the type of bird that welcomes being handled by strangers. He's not afraid to beat someone with his wings or threaten to bite off a finger. Besides, I have to lock him in his cage when I leave the van, mostly because he likes to get into mischief and tear things apart.

"He stays in a cage most of the time he's in the truck with me," I said. "But now that I know about these thefts, I'll be sure to keep him closer."

"That sounds like a good plan." Swaim glanced down at Anna, who had been steadily eating her ice cream while following our exchange like a rabid fan at a tennis match. "Miss Anna, the way that mint chocolate chip ice cream disappeared makes me think maybe I should go get some, too."

Anna flashed him a green-and-chocolate smile.

Looking back at me, he said, "It was good to see you again, Ms. Ivy. Please be sure to let me know if you see anything suspicious."

"I certainly will," I answered as we started to edge away. "And thanks for the heads up."

We crossed the parking lot and climbed into the van to find Ebony preening happily on his perch. I can't say I was surprised, but I did feel a measure of relief when I saw him still safely tucked away. I stowed our packages while Anna buckled herself into her seat, then finished the balance of my cherry vanilla cone before cranking up the engine to head home.

As we motored toward the exit, Anna said thoughtfully, "I think you probably shoulda told him about the naked man, Mama."

That girl didn't miss anything. As I mumbled my agreement, I suddenly realized I'd failed to tell him about the barking and yelping dog.

Chapter 5

My internal clock wakes me up around 5:00 a.m. every day, no matter what. This really only bothers me on cold Saturday mornings when I don't need to get up for any specific reason. Most mornings, including this one, I use the time to communicate with God. To me, there's nothing like watching the first rays of light reach through my curtains and bathe my room in their warm, earthy glow, while I'm telling the Lord how thankful I am for the blessings He has bestowed upon me.

On this specific morning, I talked a lot about Anna. I told God what an incredible person she is, and how much I value her—even when she rolls her pretty eyes at me. I specifically asked the Lord to keep her safe while she was away. The idea of her being away from me for five days brought tears to my eyes. It wasn't that we'd never spent time away from each other before— she spends time with Rex's parents a few times each year. It's just that in addition to being the center of my world, Anna is my only remaining connection to my late husband. Her absence always reminds me of the huge gaping hole in my life left by her father.

Rex and I met when we were both attending Texas Tech University. He was a very good—and very good-looking—baseball player. I have yet to figure out why—except for divine intervention—he chose me out of all the girls that flocked around him. Rex used to joke that it was my red hair that made me hard to forget, but everyone who was there that day knows the truth. It wasn't my hair or my smile, or any of the usual things. It was a towering fly ball that found its way under my foot, causing me to slip and land in a mud puddle with a splash. When he rushed to help me up, our hands touched and we each felt an instant spark. Three years later, when we decided to get married and announced our engagement, we met with resistance from both sets of parents. My father thought Rex was too flighty to provide me with a stable home; Rex's parents wanted him to marry his high school sweetheart. After the fallout that resulted from our engagement, I dropped out of school with a semester left before graduation, and we eloped. Our honeymoon was spent driving to Georgia, where Rex had to report for duty after enlisting in the Army.

Basic training burned off what little padding my husband had on his ballplayer physique. He became more muscular—a full-on hottie, in my opinion—and more focused. Rex thrived in the Army's structured environment. He loved the routine, the comradery . . . He loved everything about the Army. Rex's first deployment in Afghanistan added some seasoning to his natural good looks and gave him a more somber outlook than ever before, as though, for the first time, he was aware of his mortality. When he came back, he expressed an overwhelming desire to become a father. He was a lean, Army green sex machine, and I was a very willing participant.

Just before he was due to return to duty, he told me repeatedly that God had told him I would give birth to a girl. He even told me her name had come to him in a dream, and our daughter would be named Anna Claire. That was before I even knew I was pregnant. Sadly—devastatingly—within days of his arrival in Afghanistan, Rex was killed when his transport vehicle ran over a roadside bomb.

Soon after Rex's death, my parents and I mended our broken bonds, but I am still less than comfortable with Rex's parents, knowing that they never approved of their son's choice of wife. It was Willa Gentry who convinced me I needed to contact both sets of parents to let them know they had a new granddaughter. In their defense, the Greenes are now very polite to me, even if they aren't exactly warm and welcoming. When it comes to Anna, though, they are enthusiastic, loving grandparents who would face down the fiercest opponents bare-handed if their granddaughter was threatened. They check on Anna frequently, calling her several times a month to hear her voice and find out what she's been into. I knew the Greenes would care for my baby as though she were the most precious gift in the universe—which, of course, she is. But I also realized that, sure as the sun would set in the west, Anna's absence would feel like the vacuum at the hub of a black hole until she returned.

I heard Ebony stirring just moments before Anna padded down the hall to the bathroom. Outside my window the world was just beginning to awaken as our day truly began. I fed Ebony and both dogs while Anna got dressed and double-checked the piles of her belongings we'd set out on the dining room table. She looked on as I carefully packed her bag, checking things off the list we'd made the night before to be sure we didn't forget anything. For a brief, ridiculous moment I wondered if I could contort myself to fit in her satchel.

Although my relationship with Rex's parents has improved since (and because of) Anna Claire's arrival into the world, it's always been different with Rex's older sister, Gina, but in a good way. Gina and I have always gotten along well. Unlike her parents, she didn't have any goals for her younger brother's love life other than hoping he would find someone who made him happy. In fact, she was the only member of either of our families who was present when we married. I didn't meet her husband, Jace, until after Anna was born, and by then Gina had a baby of her own too. Cody is almost one year to the day older than Anna. It is because of Gina's intervention that I now have copies of family movies from when she and Rex were growing up, and of some of his high school baseball games. These are especially helpful when Anna has questions about her daddy or seems to feel left out that he isn't around. We occasionally meet somewhere so the kids can play, but most of Anna's exposure to this side of her family takes place while she's with her grandparents.

On this day, our rendezvous point was a travel center called Chip's, and our purpose was to meet Rex's parents for the hand-off of Anna. Rex had been born and raised in Plano, a large, bustling city north of

Dallas with all the shopping and conveniences a person could ask for without having to drive into *the* big city. His parents still live there, and Gina and her family live in nearby Murphy. The beauty of meeting at Chip's is that I don't have to drive into hectic traffic, and the Greenes don't have to leave the comfort and security of city life.

Located on Interstate 20, just outside the farthest fringes of the DFW Metroplex, the complex that houses Chip's contains so many amenities it's almost its own city. Nestled snuggly in a triangular space between I-20 and U.S. Highway 80, an entrepreneur from points unknown (to me, anyway) opened this multi-use facility to ease weary travelers. Chip's started out as a place for both professional and casual drivers to fuel their vehicles, stretch their legs, and relieve their beleaguered bladders. The feeder roads leading to and from the facility are well lit and well-marked, and the gas tends to be a few cents cheaper than what one might find closer to the Metroplex. Because of these factors, and the facility's initial offerings of gas, diesel, and clean restrooms, Chip's quickly became the favored place for people to stop before they ventured into the madness of Dallas traffic. It wasn't long before Chip's built two restaurants and a picnic area. As more people stopped, more things were added: two hotels popped up, seemingly out of nowhere, followed by a movie theatre, an RV park, and a woodland-themed playground where kids could escape the confines of the family vehicle and expend some of their pent-up energy playing among the favored places of Chip (a cartoon-style chipmunk) and his pals.

Anna loves this playground, and if I'm honest, I

have to say it *is* a lot of fun. There is a man-made oak tree with three slides coming off of it; rabbit tunnels constructed of child-sized tubes of heavy-duty plastic perforated by enormous octagonal holes, so the children are always visible; a school of over-sized fish equipped with large, industrial-strength springs so visiting kids can feel like they're riding on the backs of everything from large-mouth bass to snapping turtles. Numerous swing sets, under the cover of commercial tarps in the color of a clear blue sky, provide some relief from the sun. As an added precaution, there is even a security guard on duty during the busiest times of the day.

While we were playing on the swings, Anna tried to make me promise I wouldn't cry when she left. At this point in her life, my baby doesn't understand how impossible that is, but maybe one day she will. The best I could do was to tell her I wouldn't cry while in view of her grandparents. When the Greenes arrived, they parked their monstrous SUV on a grassy expanse across from the playground, giving them the opportunity to make something of a grand entrance. A few paces from the vehicle's front bumper, Mrs. Greene called to Anna and waved her hand as if to distinguish herself from the surrounding crowd (of which there was none). My baby girl squealed with delight and charged off to greet the newcomers. I followed, a little less enthusiastically and a degree or two slower. In truth, I always dreaded these meetings. It wasn't that I didn't like the Greenes; I just hadn't had the chance to get to know them well, given the circumstances, and wasn't at all comfortable in their presence. Fortunately, Anna didn't have this problem. The only time her excitement dimmed was when she skidded to a stop in front of them instead of launching herself into the arms of one or the other.

As I approached, Mr. Greene—who had been squatting to hug and speak to Anna—straightened and extended his hand to me in greeting. I'm always a little startled when I see Rex's parents. Mr. Greene looks so much like his late son that it would be easy to believe he'd simply been cloned. They have the same thick, curly hair, though Mr. Greene's hair has a lot more white running through it than Rex's ever did. My husband's physique might have been a little more muscular, but his athletic body type, height, walk, and smiles all came from his dad. Eye color is the only exception to this likeness trend. Mr. Greene's eyes are blue, where Rex's green came from his mother. Mrs. Greene also stood tall to greet me, the smile on her lips fading only slightly while the sincerity in her eyes all but disappeared. The hand she offered me was more along the lines of two fingers and a thumb, her touch about as welcoming as mine when I have to collect a dead rat from the floor of the chicken house. I was relieved when all the attention was once again focused on my child.

We turned as a group to make our way to the SUV. Anna skipped along between her grandparents, chattering away about the chickens and the reason she'd recently changed all of their names. At the rear door of his vehicle, Mr. Greene took the suitcase from my hand and stowed it in the back, while Mrs. Greene oohed and aahed over Anna's ability to buckle herself into her car seat. The older woman was so dramatic that I was torn between rolling my eyes and brushing away an errant tear.

I opted for the latter while Mrs. Greene was still

blocking me from Anna's view. Before the door was closed, I stepped in, hugged and kissed my baby one more time, then waved farewell as I made my way back to my own vehicle.

Once I was heading home, I stopped fighting the tears and let the flood gates fall open. I kept seeing those precious, pivotal moments of our life together: the first time I held her; her smile when she was teething and drooling; those times when she was sick and had been crying for so long that she wore herself out and fell asleep on my shoulder, even though we were both hot and sweaty; her uniquely sweet baby smell; the first time she fell face first into a mud puddle. (Most of the time it's evident that my daughter inherited her father's athletic grace, but seriously, sometimes there's no doubt the apple didn't fall far from this tree, either.) I thought about her first day of school and how proud she was when she came home with the first picture that she'd drawn. Of course, most of the things I thought about were happy memories of her sweet laugh, beautiful smile, pretty eyes, and the things that she would say to me that are just so *Anna*.

Two things helped stem the flow of my tears. The first was a text message from a client I was supposed to see Monday morning. I don't usually mess with my phone while I'm driving. I have a headset for calls, and a holder for my phone so I can read the screen without taking my eyes from the road for too many seconds. In this instance, the display remained lit long enough for me to see that this particular lady was cancelling her appointment. I thought this was odd but vowed to reschedule with her as soon as I got home.

The second distraction was an actual phone call.

"IndigoViolet, where are you?"

In case you couldn't tell by the use of my full name, it was my mother.

"I just dropped Anna off with the Greenes. Why?"

"Well, your sister is already here, and we need your help. What time do you think you'll get here?"

I had no clue what she was talking about, so I asked, "Where are you?"

"At home, of course. That's where the boxes are," Mama answered.

A dim light was beginning to flicker in my head. My mother is the dean of the biology department at Humphrey-Dearing University. She rarely teaches formal classes anymore, but she is so brilliant when it comes to things you can only see with a microscope that students line up to assist with her research. Upon the conclusion of a research project, Mother cycles all of her oldest files to her home storage facility—i.e., her garage—to make room for all of the new information she has gathered. She uses graduate assistants to haul the actual file boxes, but Win and I are required to help her sort through family mementos. Once this realization finished dawning, I knew that all the mindless responses I'd muttered while watching a naked leprechaun trot down the street had signaled my agreement to help.

"I'm sorry, Mama. I was a little distracted this morning and forgot. I'll be there in less than an hour."

My mother's voice faded slightly, indicating she had turned away to talk to Win. "Your sister says she forgot. She'd forget to put her head on in the morning if it wasn't already attached to her shoulders."

I heard my sister's throaty laugh, but her words

were muffled.

"All right, Indigo," Mama said. "Winter and I will be here, but don't dawdle. We don't have all day."

"Yes, ma'am," I answered. "Do I need to bring anything?"

My mom's heavy sigh indicated to me that she was probably shaking her head in defeat. I am, after all, the scatter-brained child.

"It'll be lunchtime by the time you get here, so you might as well pick something up for the three of us. Your daddy is at the golf course, so he'll find his own food."

I knew better than to ask if they wanted anything in particular. Instead, I agreed and disconnected the call.

As much as she loves all her children, my mother is not exactly the sentimental type—unless, of course, she's reminiscing about a particular microbe—so I didn't expect this task to take us all that long. I knew I didn't have anything there, because when I moved back to East Texas, Mama insisted I take all my stuff to my own house. Win was given a little more time to reclaim her own belongings, but I was confident that at least ninety percent of her things had been relocated. That meant that my brother's possessions would be the focus of the day's activity. Hunter had a good reason for not having had to repossess his childhood memories—he lived in a different state.

When I arrived, I flipped down the visor and surveyed my tear-streaked visage in the mirror. I gave my face a quick wipe with a tissue and pinched my cheeks to regain some color, then tried to put thoughts of Anna and my empty house out of my head. Truth told, I was grateful for the distraction. Win was seated on the floor of the garage, flanked by open boxes and presiding over a few small piles of things whose common characteristics weren't immediately clear to me. Off to her right was a huge rolling trash can that was already about half full. (Apparently, my sister inherited the indifference gene from Mama.) Coinciding with my arrival, my mother entered the garage from the direction of the house. Before acknowledging me, she surveyed the mess, peeked into the garbage can, then threw in a few items that had escaped from one of the collections.

I gave her a hug and said, "I stopped for tacos. I hope that's okay."

"Tacos are always good," Win said.

Mama nodded. "I was afraid you'd bring barbecue, and we'd have all that sauce everywhere. Let's go sit on the deck."

I helped my sister up off the floor, and we followed our mother to the glass-topped table that sits just outside of their breakfast room. I unceremoniously dumped the food in the middle, and the three of us scrambled to grab our rations as though we were expecting an eagle to swoop down and steal it from us. We then settled down to eat.

"Ivy, honey," Mama said, breaking the silence that had descended when we began to eat. She had already polished off one of the street tacos and was dressing the second before consumption. "I saw your little friend yesterday."

Now, I'm an adult, and the shortest of my friends, so whoever she was talking about was likely not all that small. I'm pretty sure I hadn't had a "little" friend since everyone else hit their growth spurt in junior high. I looked at her quizzically and asked, "What little friend?"

"You know, that boy who likes to dress up as a leprechaun."

It took me a moment to figure out who she meant. When I did, I looked up at my sister, who nonchalantly ducked her head and reached for the salsa.

"He's not my *friend*, Mama. I simply saw him running down the street."

Mother waved off my comment. "It was the funniest thing. You know I normally wouldn't have been home in the afternoon, but I came back early yesterday since all the students scattered so quickly for Spring Break. You know my neighbor, Evangeline. She was having a party with her book club in her backyard. They're usually a pretty quiet bunch, but I heard all this whooping and hollering, so I looked out this window right here and saw this boy dressed in green doing a little dance on her wall at the back of her yard. I stood there and watched for just a moment while he did his little jig. Then, in a flash, he just yanked his pants off, did a little shimmy, tipped his hat like a gentleman, jumped off the wall, and ran away."

By this time, Win and I were staring at our mother. Mama is not one to suffer foolishness, but she seemed to be genuinely entertained by this flasher.

Winter looked at her and asked, "Did you call the police?"

"Oh, heavens, no. That boy wasn't hurting anyone. He was just out there having a good time. And it was obvious that Evangeline and the gals thoroughly enjoyed the show."

I exchanged an incredulous glance with my sister.

Her expression told me I wasn't alone in being surprised that our mom hadn't chased the guy and held him for the police. I shrugged and made a move to dip a chip in the hot sauce. An instant before crunchy goodness met spicy redness, Mama smacked my hand, causing me to crush my chip on the surface of the table.

I jerked up, nearly knocking over my tea. "What was that for?!"

"That's for saying the word 'nekkid'!"

My sister giggled.

As expected, the sorting and boxing of Hunter's belongings didn't take up a lot of the afternoon. Win had been working on things before my arrival, so at least half of my brother's boxes had been opened, their contents dumped on the floor, and the appropriate items adequately dispatched. The endorphins released in our bodies by the spicy Mexican food made us punchy and too silly for our mother to tolerate, so she soon left us to finish the job. Neither Winter nor I had a committed stake in the activity, though, so it didn't take us long before we agreed to put some things in different boxes, re-tape them, and call it a day.

By the time I climbed in the pickup to go home, I had several more messages. I almost never leave my phone in the truck, especially when Anna is away. Why I did on this day is anyone's guess. At any rate, I experienced a little jolt of panic at the number of notices on my phone screen and was thus too relieved that none had to do with my daughter to worry about the reasons for the others. Maybe, subconsciously, I knew what they were, because I neglected to look at them again once I got home.

Saturdays are usually reserved for yard and housework. The lawn and flower beds were still in dormant-mode, so the only things I needed to do outside were to clean my chicken coop, play with my dogs, and hoe the plot for my vegetable garden. Inside, I needed to prep Ebony's food for the coming week and take care of some general cleaning—floors, bathroom, and laundry. I decided to stay in. Ebony needed attention after having been left alone all morning, and I could do just about everything I needed to do with him on my shoulder or supervising from one of the many perches he has throughout the house. Unsurprisingly, he is partial to helping with his food preparations, mostly because he likes to steal treats and hide them for later consumption.

By the time I had put the last of my laundry in the dryer and sat down in front of the TV to eat my sandwich supper, it was six o'clock. It was then that I looked at my phone. I had three text messages and five voice mails, all from clients, and all involving cancellations. If the trend hadn't been troubling, the voicemails would have been amusing, as they were from a lady who has a difficult time making decisions, even on a good day. Mrs. Watson is a very sweet widow in her early seventies. Although she has a tendency to be a little ditzy, she would rather show up to church in curlers and house shoes than hurt anyone's feelings. Her four-legged baby is a teacup poodle mix named Zsa Zsa, in deference to her favorite actress, Zsa Zsa Gabor. She'd called me so many times because she thought she might not want Zsa Zsa groomed this week (or month or year). To clarify, the first, third, and fifth calls were in favor of cancelling; the second and fourth were to ask if she could reinstate her original appointment.

I had a pretty good idea of why so many of my usually trustworthy clients were suddenly opting out of their slots in the grooming rotation: I had been SEEN! Seen talking with Detective Swaim while there was an active criminal operating in our town, and thus I was now the prime suspect for pet-thieving. I knew these customers weren't related by blood or by marriage, but, like everyone in our small town, they were acquainted and had probably tried and convicted me over coffee and bagels. Pinnacle's rumor mill is nothing if not efficient.

I responded to each message, acknowledging their requests and telling them I would happily reschedule their appointments if they should change their minds. Afterward, I phoned Mrs. Watson, assuring her answering machine that I harbored no hard feelings. Once that task was completed, I tossed the phone into the seat of the next chair over, tipped my head back, covered my face with my hands, and groaned.

A moment later, the sound of beating wings reached my ears, followed by Ebony's favorite greeting: "Hello, honey."

If he had been a bigger bird—sized more like a polar bear than a football—I would have hugged him. As a cockatoo, Ebony is an expert mimicker, and he has stored a wide variety of sounds in his walnut-sized brain. Since he had been raised by Willa, he most often sounded like her when he spoke in words. At that moment, her sweet voice coming from any source was a welcome balm for the pain I was feeling.

"Hello, Ebony," I answered, rubbing the feathers on

his snowy cheek. "What do you think about all these people, huh?"

My bird cocked his head to one side, slowly raised his crest feathers until they were fully extended, then cried out, "Woo-woo-woo-woo!" before cackling at himself.

I laughed too. Ebony had hit that particular nail squarely on the head.

Beside me, my phone rang, the tone indicating it was Anna. I reached for it before settling the bird in my lap for some head rubs.

"Hey, baby," I said by way of greeting.

"Hi, Mama! What are you doing?"

We made small talk for a few minutes. Anna told me about the traffic and getting to play with pizza dough at a restaurant, while I downplayed my day with the vague response that Ebony and I were "just hangin' out." In spite of her upbeat chatter, I sensed that my daughter had something on her mind, but I knew if asked, she'd likely deny it, so I waited for her to bring it up. I didn't have to wait long.

"Mama, do you know when I'm supposed to come home?" Anna's voice held more worry than sadness or loneliness.

I had no way of knowing if someone had let the Disney surprise slip out, and I didn't want to give it away if she was still in the dark about it. "What do you mean, baby? You don't miss me already, do you?"

"A little." She hesitated, likely working herself up to spitting out whatever was on her mind. "I don't think Grandmother wants me to stay here."

This was not what I expected to hear—not that I had any preconceived notions. For lack of a better option, I repeated myself. "What do you mean?"

"Well, when we got here this afternoon, I asked if I should put my clothes away in the dresser because that's what I usually do."

That's my kid: efficient, organized, and polite. Had it been me at that age, I would have dropped my suitcase next to the nearest wall and run outside to see what mischief I could get into.

Her voice trembling, Anna continued, "Grandmother told me not to take anything out of my suitcase. Not one thing."

These last three words, spoken in my daughter's sweet, lilting voice, brought a smile to my face. I knew Mrs. Greene could be abrupt, so I understood why Anna was feeling the way she was.

"Did you ask her why?"

"No. I was afraid if I did, she'd make me get back in the car, and we'd go straight home, and I didn't want that. Cody was telling me about his skateboard, and I want to stay here long enough to try it out."

I had to bite my lip to keep from chuckling.

"I can understand that," I said. "But why would you think your grandmother would make you come home already? Were you behaving yourself?"

"I think so. It was before we went to eat pizza, and I wasn't the one who threw my dough up in the air to see if it would stick to the ceiling." Anna paused to sigh heavily while I swallowed a laugh. When she continued, she said, "I don't think Grandmother likes me very much."

"Oh, baby, I guarantee she does like you—she loves you a whole bunch."

"Then, why was she mad? Why doesn't she want

me to stay here?" My typically level-headed child sounded like she was about to burst into tears.

"Anna," I said as gently as I could, "sometimes people feel things that have nothing to do with us. Sometimes other things happen that we don't notice. I'm sure that if your grandmother was angry, she wasn't angry with you—unless there's something you aren't telling me."

"No, Mama! I promise!"

"Okay, baby, calm down. I'm sure she has a good reason for not wanting you to unpack your suitcase, and I know she isn't ready to send you home, yet."

"How do you know?"

"Well, for one thing, if Grandmother Greene wanted to send you home, she would have called me to let me know, and she hasn't called."

"And you had your phone with you?"

"Yes." In general, I'm a terrible liar, and I especially hate lying to my child. In this case, however, I was confident I could get by. "Other people called me today, so I know it was working, but neither your grandmother nor your grandfather called."

Anna sighed again, but when she spoke, her voice was brighter. "Okay. Do you think I should go ahead and put my things away?"

I hesitated. Their flight was scheduled to take off around mid-morning tomorrow. Herding a six-year-old can be challenging for someone who isn't accustomed to it, even if the child is an easy kid. Add to that having to repack a suitcase, and the morning could turn into a disaster in the blink of an eye. "Why don't you hold off on that? Your clothes aren't going to mind sleeping in the suitcase."

Anna giggled. "You're silly, Mama."

"Yes, but I got to hear you laugh."

Another chuckle escaped before she asked, "Did you cry when you left me today?"

"I did, but just for a little bit," I admitted.

"Do you miss me already?"

"Of course, I do! I miss you like I'd miss the sun if it didn't come up tomorrow."

"Did you remember your favorite Bible sentence?"

It was my turn to sigh . . . and hedge. "Well, as I told you before, I don't think I have just *one* favorite Bible verse. There are a bunch that I really like."

"But . . ."

"But," it was my turn to interrupt, "I will think about it all night tonight, and I'll have an idea for you tomorrow. How does that sound?"

"Okay," Anna answered, sounding relieved. "I have to go, Mama. Grandfather said we can have ice cream, and I can't eat it and talk at the same time. I love you, Mama."

And with that, she was gone.

Chapter 6

You know how it is when you have to be somewhere and you have plenty of time to get ready, but somehow you still manage to be late?

That was me on Sunday morning. I didn't have to worry about getting Anna up, dressed, and fed before church. I woke at five o'clock as usual, took a shower, and lingered in the sunroom, just watching the sun come up and rubbing Ebony's scrawny little birdy neck. I got lost in the beauty of the morning, with the early light sifting through the leaves, dappling the lawn outside my window.

I'm not sure exactly what it was that drew my attention to the time, but I soon realized I'd been sitting there too long. In fact, I had only about forty-five minutes to feed all the animals, finish putting on suitable clothes, and get to church. Fortunately, the first thing I touched in my closet was a simple long-sleeved dress with green leaves on a white background—perfect for spring. It was warm enough for a chilly morning, and it made me feel like I looked really cute. I put Ebony back in his cage, grabbed a granola bar for breakfast, and charged out the door, barely managing to keep from breaking the sound barrier on my way into town. I was in such a hurry when I finally did get to the church that, by the time I got to our family pew, I was panting and sweating canine-style. My father is all-too familiar with my behavior, especially my penchant for losing track of time. He shook his head, not bothering to comment as he stood to let me pass so I could sit next to him.

Within moments of our pastor beginning his sermon, my mind wandered. I thought of Anna's school assignment and realized that I needed to find something for her. I picked up the Bible that rested in a holder on the back of the pew in front of me and flipped to a section I always enjoy. It took me a minute to find it because it is in the Book of Job, and there are forty-two chapters about that particular man and his trials. Finally, I located what I was looking for: Job 39. At this point in the story, God is questioning Job about the creatures on the earth, who made them, who gave them their strengths and their individual characteristics. My favorite part of this begins with verse 19:

> "Hast thou given the horse strength? Hast thou clothed his neck with thunder? Canst thou make him afraid as a grasshopper? The glory of his nostrils is terrible.
>
> He paweth in the valley, and rejoiceth in his strength: he goeth on to meet the armed men.
>
> He mocketh at fear, and is not affrighted; neither turneth he back from the sword.
>
> The quiver rattleth against him, the glittering spear and the shield.
>
> He swalloweth the ground with fierceness

and rage: neither believeth he that it is the sound of the trumpet.

He saith among the trumpets, Ha, ha; and he smelleth the battle afar off, the thunder of the captains, and the shouting."

This passage initially caught my attention because it involves a horse. I love the imagery of a gallant steed chomping at the bit, ready to carry his warrior into battle before emerging victorious. The problem is that it's a pretty long passage, and it seemed like a lot to expect a six-year-old to use all that flowery language to describe a horse going into battle.

Since I wasn't paying much attention to the sermon anyway, I decided to see if I could find a more suitable passage, one that was both meaningful and relatively easy for Anna to grasp. Employing the classic "flip and point" method, I shut the Bible, closed my eyes, and flipped to a random page before sticking my finger to the paper and looking down. I'd landed in the Old Testament, Jeremiah 29, verse 11. It read, "For I know the thoughts that I think toward you, saith the LORD, thoughts of peace, and not of evil, to give you an expected end."

That was pretty good, and I thought it actually had the potential for Anna to memorize now and maybe apply to her life as she grows older. I hesitated, though, because I don't know how many kids think about plans for the future beyond what flavor of ice cream they want to order for dessert, or how many pets they would have when they grow up (three dogs, two cats, one pony, and an aquarium full of exotic fish). The concept of "future" is hard enough for some adults.

I closed the book again and went through the same procedure. When I next opened the Bible, I was in Timothy. It was Second Timothy, chapter 1, verse 7: "For God hath not given us the spirit of fear; but of power, and of love, and of a sound mind." Not bad, but I can't say that Anna is timid, or that I want to encourage her to be any less shy. And while it's never too soon to learn about self-discipline, I wasn't sure if a few days would be long enough for her to feel comfortable with discussing it in class.

The next time I opened the Bible, I found myself looking at Deuteronomy chapter 31, verse 6: "Be strong and of a good courage, fear not, nor be afraid of them: for the Lord thy God, he it is that doth go with thee; he will not fail thee nor forsake thee." There was a lot of meaning in that one, and maybe I could shorten it. Then again, Anna is already strong and courageous. I wasn't sure I needed to encourage more of that.

I went back to the drawing board. After repeating my less-than-technical procedure several more times, I realized that most of the passages had to do with strength and courage, and I wondered what exactly God was trying to tell me. The glare from my father sitting next to me was a lot easier to interpret—he wanted me to stop rifling through pages when I was supposed to be hanging on to the pastor's every word.

A few moments later, Daddy dug an elbow in my side before he got to his feet. I quickly realized the rest of the congregation was standing and followed suit. Apparently, I'd flipped and pondered through the entire sermon, and it was now time to sing a final hymn before the service was over. I slipped the Bible back in its resting spot and began to sing.

Chapter 7

We don't have a rigid Sunday routine in my family, but we do have an informal schedule. Typically, sometime between crawling out of bed, getting dressed, and eating breakfast, Anna and I throw some casual clothes in a bag before heading out for church where we meet up with my dad, and Winter and her family. The kids are deposited in their respective Sunday school rooms while those of us who more closely resemble grown-ups wade into the sanctuary for the weekly worship service. My mother isn't a fan of attending church. She acknowledges the existence of God but says she prefers to commune with Him in her own way. Because of her absence, once the service is over, Daddy leaves to pick her up before we all reassemble at Winter's house for a family dinner. We're usually there for most of the day, which gives all the kids—including some of us who are chronologically adults—a chance to be children together.

This Sunday would be different for a number of reasons. Anna, of course, was absent, so there was one less bubbly laugh in my sister's household.

Additionally, I'd forgotten to grab my change of clothes, so I'd be forced to remain a grown-up until I returned home later in the day.

As is typical, Mother and I were helping Winter with meal preparations when my phone rang. Win was doing whatever she does with the main course to make it smell and taste heavenly—today it was a pot roast, cooked in the oven. Mama was assembling the family's homemade vinaigrette with the precision of a molecular engineer (which is, of course, one of her many skills) while I was cutting up fruit for dessert. Everyone was busy, and my hands were messy, so I hesitated to answer. The phone continued to ring while I leaned over to check the caller ID.

"Answer the phone already, Ivy," Mother commanded. "Or turn the stupid thing off. I'll never understand why you can't have a phone that just rings, instead of playing that ridiculous noise."

Okay, to be clear, whenever someone calls my mother's phone, everyone in a two-mile radius is serenaded by a Bach sonata. By contrast, my ringer is a little more fun—it's something silly Anna and I downloaded called "Hip-Hop Cows." It starts with a couple of bass drum thumps, followed by a long and deep *mooo* that is accompanied by an electric guitar. Most people find it vastly entertaining—even to the point of asking for my number so they can call me and hear it again—but Mama isn't most people, and she can't stand it.

The name on the screen was L. Swaim, so I decided to answer it in spite of the uncomfortable feeling that was gnawing at the pit of my stomach. I used my knuckle to pick up the call and put it on speaker. For people I know well, I usually answer the phone with "Hey!" Client calls are greeted with, "Hi, this is Ivy," and others generally get the standard "Hello?" I'm never really sure where I stand with The Swami, so when I answered this time, it was more along the lines of "He-ey-lo."

Winter snorted somewhere off to my left.

"Well, good morning, Ms. Ivy. This is Luke Swaim. How are you this fine Sunday?"

Before I could form an answer, Win shouted, "Who'd you kill this time, sis?"

Several months ago, shortly after Detective Swaim moved to Pinnacle, I discovered a dead body in one of our city parks. The deceased was a man known to many people—and, incidentally, liked by few—in our community. Since I was the one who reported it, and somehow everyone in town seemed to recall the ridiculous threat I'd made against the man when I was ten, I was briefly investigated as a possible suspect. I was cleared, of course, with the help of the childhood-bully-turned-desperate-psycho who not only proved to be the actual killer but also broke into my home in an attempt to silence me permanently.

I shot my sister a scorching glare, and I answered. "In case you couldn't tell, detective, you're on speaker. My mother and sister are here with me."

"Well, hello, ladies!" The Swami has a voice that can hypnotize an unsuspecting female even over the phone. "I hope you are enjoying this beautiful day."

"Well, no one is dead yet, so we've had a good start," Mama answered, picking up where my sister left off.

The detective chuckled while I contemplated

committing a crime for real using the two-inch paring knife in my hand.

In hopes of moving the conversation along, I asked, "And how are you today, detective?"

"Aww, I'm better than a basket full of baby chicks in a barrel full of earthworms."

From the corner of my eye, I saw both Mama and Win turn around, each wearing the same bewildered look I was surely sporting.

I wasn't sure if a barrel full of worms would be a pleasant thing for any living creature, so I tried a different question. "So, how can I help you, Detective Swaim? Did you get a dog?"

"No, ma'am," he answered with another chuckle. "I was just hoping I could get a little of your time today, maybe this afternoon, to have a conversation."

"What kind of conversation?" I asked guardedly.

"Oh good grief, Ivy," Mama retorted. "The man is only asking to see you. I seriously doubt he's planning to strap you to a chair and bludgeon you with a nightstick."

Win giggled. I closed my eyes and asked God to give me patience with my family. Then I clutched my knife even more tightly.

"Oh, you know, Ms. Ivy, I just want to pick your brain a little bit."

Slightly encouraged, I said, "Oh good, you're planning on getting a dog. There are several breeds that would make a great companion for a man such as you."

This time, Swaim's chuckle was a little less comfortable. "Well, to tell you the truth, ma'am, that isn't the part of your brain I wanted to pick."

Behind me, Win uttered a dramatic gasp before

doing her vocal imitation of foreboding music. "Dun-dun-duuuuunnnn."

"Just for clarification purposes, is this the kind of conversation my dad would find interesting in a professional sense, or from a strictly paternal point of view?" I asked.

I could hear Mama mutter, "Oh, very good question IndigoViolet."

The detective paused before saying, "You might say he'd find it intriguing from a legal perspective."

I suppressed a heavy sigh, looked over my shoulder, and yelled, "Daddy!"

Chapter 8

Two hours later my father and I walked into the
Pinnacle Police Department building. Since I'd left my
Sunday afternoon clothes on the arm of my couch and
Win lived on the exact opposite end of town from me, I
was still wearing my church clothes. Given that we live
in the piney woods of East Texas, I was overdressed for
a voluntary visit to the police station, even if it was a
Sunday. Most of the police force know my dad, either
because he's been an instructor for one of their
academy classes or because they've seen him in court.
I'm almost as well known, but for different reasons:
either because I drive a huge, lavender-painted van, or
because I was the subject of more than one BOLO (be
on the lookout for) during the aforementioned murder
investigation.

In other words, if anyone was surprised to see us in
the department's lobby that afternoon, it didn't show.

Daddy and I were led to a room with a battered
wood table, four chairs, and a single window that
overlooked the impound yard. It wasn't precisely an

interrogation room—those had two-way mirrors instead of a window (don't ask me how I know this)—but it wasn't Swaim's office, either. The detective came in just a few moments after us and offered water or coffee before he'd completely cleared the doorway. We each declined, and he invited us to have a seat.

"I just have some general questions for you today, Ms. Ivy. With your permission, I'd like to record our session." He pointed to a small digital recorder that seemed to have appeared out of thin air.

"Why?" I asked.

Swaim grinned. "Well, it saves time on both ends. For you, it means you don't have to wait for me to write down your answers, and for me, it means I don't have to spend extra time deciphering my own handwriting."

I shrugged.

He took that to mean "yes" and switched on the device. After stating his name, the date and time, and our names, Swaim said, "Now, this is nothing more than an informal question session. You aren't under arrest or anything, but if you'd like, I can advise you of your rights before we go any further."

"Under the circumstance, I think that would be a good idea," Daddy answered for me.

Swaim nodded and began reciting the Miranda Rights. I made a mental note to ask my dad who Miranda was and what she could have done to inspire such a statement.

"Do you understand these rights as they've been read to you, ma'am?"

Feeling a little fuzzy, I nodded.

"I'll need you to tell me either 'yes' or 'no,' for the benefit of the recording," he prodded.

"Yes," I answered, unexpectedly breathless.

"Very good," he responded, as he looked down at his notes. "Ms. Greene, can you tell me where you were on the following dates and times?"

He read off four dates, including the day of the week and a time frame for each.

"I need to check my calendar," I answered, holding up my phone. When he spoke his affirmation, I opened the calendar app and gave him the information I had on my whereabouts.

"Do you have any proof—receipts, photos, or any kind of written documentation—to support the information you've just provided?"

"I have signed receipts for the three instances where I was with a client, but those are on my tablet at home. I would have to email you a copy of each. For the fourth time, I was picking up Anna. It was after school, so I didn't have to sign her out."

"Did anyone see you picking up your daughter that day?"

"I'm sure several people saw me, but since this is something I do almost every day during the school week, I don't know that I can be specific about which people saw me."

"All right, Ms. Greene," Swaim said affably. "If we need to interview anyone, we can always ask you for a list at a later date. Let's move on."

From there, the detective asked me a series of questions about my job, including general information about the steps I follow when bathing and grooming a dog. He asked about my relationships with my clientele and their pets and how I feel about being a dog groomer. I answered every question as calmly as possible while Daddy sat in silence next to me, only occasionally nodding his head in encouragement.

After a time, the detective said, "Let's change the subject just a little bit. You said you have a daughter. What is her name and age?"

My inner mother grizzly awoke. "Well, since you've met her, you know her name is Anna Claire, and she's six years old."

"So her full name is Anna Claire Greene? G-r-e-e-n-e and not G-r-u-e-n-e?"

"That's correct."

"And G-r-e-e-n-e is the correct spelling of her father's last name?"

"Yes . . ." My concerned confusion made me draw out my three-letter answer.

"I don't believe I've met her father. Does he live here in Pinnacle?"

"We've had this conversation before, Detective Swaim. Anna's father—my husband—was killed in Afghanistan before Anna was born. You've seen the pictures on my living room wall. What, exactly, is this about?"

My dad patted my arm gently in an effort to calm the bear growling inside me.

"I'm just filling in some background details, ma'am." He broke eye contact with me and glanced at his notes. "What branch of the armed services did your husband serve in?"

"He was in the Army, part of the 11th Infantry unit. He had just started his second deployment when he was killed."

"And how did he die, ma'am?"

"An IED . . . an improvised explosive device that

was triggered when the truck he was riding in drove over it."

"Was your husband the only man killed, or were there survivors?"

Dredging up old memories was adding emotion to the stress of the situation. I was fighting both tears and anger. "Excuse me? What difference does that make?"

"I'm just trying to be thorough, Ms. Greene. This is in the interest of not making you have to come in a second time to answer background questions."

Finally, Daddy sat forward and spoke. "Detective, we've been rather patient this afternoon, but I feel it is my duty to ask what compels you to follow this line of questioning. I would appreciate it if you would explain to me why you asked to interview my client today."

I felt a touch of victory at being referred to as *my client*. This meant my dad had shed his parental cloak and was now in full attorney mode.

"Mr. Gruene, there have been a number of thefts in the area in the last several weeks. Someone has been stealing people's pets, sometimes by breaking into their homes. The dollar amount in terms of damage to property and the value assigned to these animals—many of which have pedigrees and are registered with the appropriate breed group—has reached the point where we have to investigate it as a possible felonious action. Your daughter is in a unique position to know the locations of and have access to each of the missing pets. At this point in my investigation, I'm simply trying to pin down the likelihood of Ms. Greene's involvement. My questions will most likely eliminate her as a suspect, but we won't know until we have all the information."

"Thank you, detective. You may proceed." With that, my father patted my arm again and sat back in his chair.

I'm sure the look I gave him betrayed the utter bafflement and fury I felt at being subjected to a grilling by a man who surely knew me well enough to understand I was no pet-napper.

"Now, where were we?" Swaim asked.

"You were trying to see if there were any witnesses to my husband's death," I said hostilely. "The answer is *yes*, there was a truck following the one Rex was in, but I don't have their names or current locations. I don't have any information on the people who planted the bomb, either. And to answer your original question, no one in that particular truck survived."

The room was quiet for a few moments. Swaim had the grace to look pained at my answer, but he resumed his professional façade when he looked up from his notes once again.

"Ms. Greene, do you receive a monthly stipend from the Army as a survivor benefit?"

"No."

"Can you tell me how much income you earn on an average monthly basis? And do you have tax records at your disposal to support your claims?"

"As a small business owner, I have to keep meticulous, detailed records of my income and expenses. I don't have those with me at this time, but I can supply them if I have to. Listen Luke—I mean, detective—don't you think I would have to be pretty stupid to steal pets from current and potential clients in a town where everyone knows everything about everyone else? That would be like cutting off my nose to spite my face."

Swaim smiled with his mouth, but not his eyes. "Well, Ms. Greene, I personally don't see how the theft of pets could be that lucrative, but then I'm not the one stealing them. However, while I don't know how good an income there is to be made as a dog groomer—mobile or otherwise—I do know that the tuition for your daughter's private school can't be cheap. In addition, you live in a home that is not a rental property, you drive a large vehicle for your work that had to have been expensive to outfit and convert, and you own an expensive exotic bird. It's hard for me to imagine that you were able to obtain a loan for your business so soon after you returned to the area and with nothing to offer as collateral. With all of this in mind, I began to wonder how you are able to afford all these extravagances on a dog groomer's salary. I ran a report on your financials for the last few months. It indicated you received an electronic deposit in the amount of four thousand dollars from an unidentified source listed only as *Gentry Trust*. So, please, Ms. Greene, enlighten me. Where have you gotten all your money?"

I felt my face grow hot, though it wasn't due to embarrassment. My anger was also causing my vision to narrow and spots to pop up in my eyes. When I looked down to dig in my purse once again, I'm pretty sure I saw steam coming from my nostrils as I exhaled.

I pulled a worn business card from the back of my wallet and a pen, which I used to write a number on the back. When finished, I did my best to remain calm as I put the pen and my phone back in my purse, placed the card on the table, and stood. My fury was making me tremble.

"On the back of that card is the number for the Army's survivor benefits line. I'm sure they can answer any questions you might have about the lump-sum death benefit payment that was made upon my husband's death. On the front of the card, you will find information for the gentleman who administers the Gentry Trust. His name is Albert Daniel. He's an attorney in the state of Georgia. I have no doubt that he can *enlighten* you about the quarterly deposits I receive from that trust." In anger, I spun around on my heel, knocking my chair back several feet. I stepped around it, stomped to the door, and started down the hall, tossing, "Are you coming, Daddy?" over my shoulder as I left.

Chapter 9

I dropped my father off at their house and went home to stew. With the help of Daddy's reassurances and parting hug, I was almost calm by the time I got there, but the sight and sound of Ebony set me off again. Swaim had been way out of line in his manner of questioning. I hadn't expected his questions to be sweet and inviting, but I never thought he would be one to ask for the gory details of Rex's death or imply that I had been less than truthful about Anna's parentage. His tone on the phone had been friendly, even comical, with that reference to the baby chicks, but that pretense disappeared as soon as we crossed the threshold of that horrible little room.

"And what's with the whole *Ms. Greene* thing, anyway?" I shouted to my empty living room. "What happened to *Ms. Ivy?*"

I growled and flopped down on the couch, only to bounce up again and start pacing. One minute The Swami is all *aw, shucks ma'am* and the next he's grilling me like a cheap steak. I thought we were friends! But no! The tiniest suspicion, the mere hint of a rumor, and suddenly he acts like I'm a complete stranger.

"That's me," I complained out loud, "Ivy Greene, public enemy number one!"

Ebony emitted a birdy laugh, then fluffed himself from his head to the tip of his tail, effectively popping my bubble of anger. I sighed and scooped him up from the arm of the couch before going off to change my clothes. Instead of staying inside and shouting my frustrations at the ceiling only to have them bounce right back, I decided to go outside and work in my garden. I needed a healthy way to work off my emotions.

I needed space to think about the Gentry Trust.

I was about four months pregnant when Willa Gentry and Ebony had found me sitting alone on a park bench, crying. I was young and scared, and they helped me find my way through the darkness of Rex's death. Since I wasn't talking to my parents at the time, I couldn't speak to my mother about the changes my body was experiencing, and I had no one who would listen to my memories concerning my husband as I worked through my grief—until Willa stepped in and took care of me. I lived with her and Ebony for about three and a half years. At first, it was at her insistence, but later, I stayed because the four of us—Willa, Ebony, Anna, and I—were happy together.

I never met Colonel Gentry, but from what his widow told me, he was a warm-hearted man with quite a sense of humor. For her part, Willa was also extremely kind and loving, always happy to help out people in any way she could. Together, they created and raised three children—two boys and a girl—who went on to have families of their own.

I had the opportunity to meet the Gentry children and their offspring only twice. The first time was when I planned a surprise party for Willa's ninetieth birthday. I called their daughter Sherry, hoping she would help spread the word about the party. What I got was completely unexpected: a tyrant who took over. Sherry told me what kind of cake to order, the types of food to serve, and the number of guests we could expect. At first, I gave her the benefit of the doubt, thinking that Willa's kids would undoubtedly know her likes better than I. When all three families arrived, however, I discovered that the Gentry children had grown up to be selfish, entitled adults with kids of their own who were disrespectful, lazy, and mean. The adults treated Willa like an invalid who'd lost all common sense, and the only time they acknowledged me was when issuing orders for something to be fetched or served. The grandchildren ran through the house tearing things up and tormenting Ebony whenever the opportunity presented itself. The poor bird spent much of the time clinging desperately to either Willa or me in an effort to stay clear of the little demons. I protected Ebony as well as I could, but Willa seemed so happy to see everyone that I didn't think she noticed the negative side-effects.

A little more than two years later, shortly after Anna and I had returned from a trip to see my parents, Willa passed away. I was boiling water for tea early one morning when I heard Ebony making a lot of noise. His cage was kept in Willa's room. Since she had been looking tired, I rushed in to try to keep him from waking her. I used the light from the hallway to unlock and open his cage, but when I reached in to get him, he flew past me and perched on Willa's hip. Knowing something was wrong, I turned on the light. She wasn't moving, wasn't breathing, and her skin was cool to the touch. It didn't take a rocket scientist to realize Willa had passed away during the night. When I again tried to collect Ebony, he hopped to the bed and waddled up to the pillow in front of his human mother's face. He leaned in close to her, turning his head this way and that, before reaching out to touch his tongue to her cheek. Birds frequently use their tongues to feel things in much the same way as humans use their fingers. Ebony wasn't licking Willa's skin; he was simply reaching out to touch her. I watched the bird, unable to fully comprehend what he was doing and incapable of stopping him. Just before he flew over to perch on my shoulder, Ebony muttered, "Bye-bye."

We returned to the kitchen, where the teapot was whistling away. I knew I needed to call someone but had no idea who that should be. I was worried that if I called 911, I'd be arrested for allowing Willa to die, and Anna would be placed in foster care until I was cleared. Eventually, my mind settled on the right person to call. Over the years, Willa had told me repeatedly that if anything ever happened to her, I was to get in touch with her lawyer. It took a little while, but Ebony and I eventually found his number in Willa's address book and, in spite of the early hour, called him.

I liked Willa's lawyer friend from the first time I'd met him. His name was Albert Daniel, and he looked like the quintessential, old-time southern gentleman. He wore three-piece suits with understated ties and highly polished, black shoes. His hair and mustache were meticulously trimmed. He carried a walking cane though I don't think he actually needed it—and always smelled lightly of cologne and quality cigars. A bit like Clark Gable with white hair. I'd had occasion to meet him several times while living with Willa and having him around at the time of her death was a blessing of immense proportion. The only law Mr. Daniel still practiced was to oversee the last wishes of his clients as they preceded him to the next life. I expect he was at least eighty, but the man's mind was as sharp as anyone's half his age.

To make a long story short, other calls were made, Willa's family came in, and Anna and I were kicked to the curb. Sherry maintained that we had no business staying in *her* house, even though it was the only home Anna had ever known. She even employed her own teenaged boys to watch as we packed to make sure we didn't steal anything.

At first, the family refused to let Ebony come with me. Before I left, I settled him in his cage and tried to reassure him it would be okay, all the while worrying about what would happen to him without my protection. Sherry closed Willa's bedroom door behind me, after which not one of the people who'd planned to stay overnight gave a second thought to Ebony until he started screeching.

If you've never been around a bird larger than a canary, you wouldn't understand the sounds an unhappy bird can make or how loud they can get. Just like the poop that comes out the back end, the volume and number of objections that come out the frontend increase with the size of the bird. He made noise—a *lot* of noise—and, not knowing what else to do, they tried to appease him by letting him out.

Ebony was accustomed to having the run of the house and getting a lot of attention from people who at least *liked* him. But that night, trapped in a house with seven people who'd done nothing but torment him in the past, Ebony unleashed a fury so intense, so unbridled, he was like a rapacious raptor pursuing his prey. He flew at people's heads, screaming loud enough to make their ears ring. He knocked full cups of coffee and large glasses of iced tea off tables. He pooped on people, their possessions, and their meals, and basically wreaked havoc that none could have previously imagined. When they were finally able to throw a blanket over him and lock him in his cage, Ebony alternately shrieked like a banshee and barked like each of the four Ivories in his past. When the group could take no more of the ear-splitting noise, they carried his cage out to the gazebo—no small feat considering the pen itself was five feet tall, five feet wide, four feet deep, didn't have castors, and had a belligerent bird with a sharp beak inside. But it only got worse from there: once outside in the dark, Ebony proceeded to wail and cry like a neglected newborn baby. (As best as I can tell, he picked up the cries and wails from baby Anna, though she was never, ever, left alone or neglected.)

Concerned neighbors raised the alarm first and phoned the police, followed by those within the surrounding zip codes who were irritated at having their sleep interrupted. Mr. Daniel phoned me shortly after 1:00 a.m., asking that I please go collect the bird. Ebony quieted as soon as he heard my pickup in the driveway, then he docilely hopped onto my shoulder and went back to the hotel with us. Thus, peace was restored.

Mr. Daniel kept me informed about the memorial service. His wife babysat Anna and Ebony while he escorted me to the church. An enormous crowd turned out for the service, some I'd met in passing but most of whom I hadn't. As Mr. Daniel and I sat in the back of the chapel, we were able to overhear the anecdotes of love and generosity many of the attendees shared with each other. It was a beautiful service, one which Willa herself had organized in her later years. At the front of the chapel, serving as a focal point for the mourners, sat an enlarged picture that I had taken of Willa the previous summer. In the photo Willa was smiling at the camera from her vegetable garden, Ebony perched happily on her shoulder and Anna at her side. The original photo hangs in my own living room to this day. After the service, I heard someone ask Sherry about the child in the picture. Her response was, "It's just some kid."

I hung around Columbus for about another two weeks. I'd made arrangements to move in with my parents back in Pinnacle, but I had to be sure of Ebony's future. At Mr. Daniel's urging, I attended the reading of my good friend's last will. I endured enough piercing looks from the family that I was a little surprised I didn't bleed to death. A brief inventory of the estate was read, including the market appraisal of the house and the current value of Willa's various investments. Mr. Daniel then read a statement specifying which assets were to be assigned to which person. The bedroom furniture used by both Anna and me were to be given to us along with a few small items that were little more than knick-knacks of common interest among the three of us. A final disbursement notation was read after a pregnant pause. Mr. Daniel wanted the family's complete attention to ensure there would be no confusion as to the details Willa had set forth when it came to the care of her most prized possession.

I had mistakenly thought this wonderful woman had turned a blind eye to the actions of her kin. Instead, she used a letter—read to us by her lawyer—to itemize the numerous times one of the group had tried to pull out Ebony's feathers, thrown something intended to spook him, or attempted to feed him something that was poisonous to birds. It was in this message that Willa declared the bulk of her savings would go for Ebony's care, hoping to ensure that her beloved pet lived a long, happy, and healthy life.

The actual dollar amount was staggering, and I could see the visions of personal wealth reflected in the eyes of her family in the room. Those dreams were quickly extinguished when Mr. Daniel named me as Ebony's custodial caretaker, followed by the name of a specific sanctuary for exotic domesticated birds should I decide I didn't want the burden of his care.

The outrage at this directive was overwhelming. It wasn't that anyone wanted Ebony—in fact, one of the grandchildren joked that a cockatoo was barely big enough to eat. What they all wanted, of course, was the money. They threatened to contest the will until they found a judge who would rule in their favor, or they were all broke, whichever came first.

Ebony moved back to Texas with Anna and me.

Using some of the money from Rex's death benefits, I bought our house, then purchased and outfitted my work van. A month or so later, Mr. Daniel called to tell me that Willa's surviving family had agreed that Ebony's inheritance should be held in a trust with quarterly disbursements for his care, provided I supplied quarterly expense reports and semi-annual wellness checks by an avian vet *not* located in my immediate area.

Now you might be wondering how in the world a person can spend more than a thousand dollars a month on a bird. Trust me, it would be a cinch even if a percentage of monthly utilities weren't included. The treat puzzles I buy to keep Ebony challenged, the fresh fruits and vegetables I provide him, and the perches he loves to shred don't come cheap. Even so, I don't use all of the quarterly disbursements. Ebony has his own savings account in the event that one of the remaining Gentrys finds a way around the trust agreement.

As painful as all these memories are for me, they are not what made me so angry on this particular Sunday afternoon. Granted, my family knew nothing of Ebony's trust fund. I didn't think it was anyone's business, and I'd had no intention of telling them unless or until something happened to put me out of commission, and someone else had to take over raising Anna. No, what truly angered me was the fact that Detective Swaim had felt the need to question Rex's death as background in the investigation.

During the first twelve years of my life, I lived in the tiny town of East, Texas. With the introduction of a new century, East and several other small towns in the area joined together to create the community of Pinnacle. I graduated from Pinnacle High School, somewhere in the middle of a class of about two hundred students. In the time before I left for college, most of the people in the newly consolidated city knew me either through the school, because of my part-time job at the grocery store, or because my parents were employed by Humphrey-Dearing University. Even with the six little towns coming together to form the larger municipality of Pinnacle, it was still, essentially, a small town.

I went to college in Lubbock on the complete opposite end of our enormous state. That's where I met Rex, and we spent most of our time in that locale until he joined the Army and we moved to Georgia. The few times we did return to East Texas as a couple, the only people who really saw us were my family. Rex and I were married by the Justice of the Peace in Lubbock. Only our closest friends were invited. It was almost three years before my parents even knew where we'd landed, much less that we were married. In other words, when Anna and I moved back from Georgia, all anyone saw was a young, seemingly unmarried woman with a child. Most people simply assumed I'd gotten pregnant, was dumped by my boyfriend, and crawled home to Mommy and Daddy hoping they would help me raise my illegitimate daughter. The fact that I own my own home and have a successful business is irrelevant. The town may have grown since I'd moved away, but the foundation of our little berg remained the same: a group of older people considered to be the bedrock of the community, very much fixed in their old-fashioned ways, who had little else to do but mind other people's business.

For those who most enjoy gossip, the truth is nowhere near as exciting as fiction.

So, there I was in my backyard on a chilly Sunday afternoon in March, hacking away at the dirt in my vegetable garden, taking out my anger at Pinnacle's smallest minds by hoeing rows in the soil. I won't say I was swearing, but I was definitely zoned in on my own thoughts and frequently muttering to myself. I was so focused, so utterly oblivious to the world outside of my head, that when a hand landed on my shoulder, I screamed, turned, and almost bludgeoned my neighbor with a hoe handle. "Whoa!" was the first word that penetrated my brain.

James Williamson.

I'd had the biggest crush on him when he dated my sister in high school. It had been one of those all-consuming infatuations where I couldn't eat, couldn't sleep, prayed I'd see him for even a second, then prayed I wouldn't. Part of my infatuation was his "bad boy" vibe, part was because he was because he would speak to me like a person whenever he saw me (which was not something many of Winter's boyfriends did). I'm not ashamed to admit I still harbor a small fraction of those romantic delusions. My heart still does a little flutter when I look into those blue-green eyes that seem to change color depending on what he's wearing. He's lost his dark mystique, and my daddy no longer wants to plant him in an unmarked grave, but James still has an intoxicating smile. A mechanic by trade, his line of work has kept him physically fit. And even though his light brown hair is just beginning to show a little gray at the temples, I have to say he's even more attractive now with some age on him than he was when he was younger.

"Oh, hey, James," I said, turning around to face him. "What're you doing here?"

He glanced from my face to my feet and back again then scratched his head. "Well, I was coming to see if you wanted to go grab some supper since you're on your own tonight. Then I heard you talking and found you over here hacking up the ground. You looked kind of like a squirrel on crack trying to find last year's acorn. What's going on?"

I sighed and shifted my feet. Of course, being that I'm not terribly graceful, I managed to twist my ankle in the freshly turned soil. As I righted myself and tried to cover my wince, I shrugged, sighed, and said, "Oh, you know, small town life, small town minds."

James shook his head. "After the damage you've done here, you're going to have to be a little more specific."

I looked around at the dirt I'd recently attacked. Any weeds that had been there before were now tiny pieces of mulch. I sighed again. "It's kind of a long story."

Taking the hoe from my hand, he said, "Well, if you'll go in and get cleaned up, I'm sure you'll have plenty of time to tell me on the way to Carthage."

I nodded and started to hobble toward my house. After a few steps, I turned back to him. "Why Carthage?"

Chuckling, James said, "Nobody will know us there, so there won't be any more gossip, and you can relax."

JUDGE NOT

Chapter 10

"Oh, Mama! Guess where I am! You'll never guess—I'll have to tell you! I'm at Disney World!"

My cellphone rang just as I was walking into the house after supper. During the forty-five-mile drive with James to eat take-out chicken, I had vented all of my anger and frustrations over being the primary focus of the local gossip mill. I felt better for it, a little lighter, and ready to hear all about my girl's special day.

Anna was so excited her voice was at least two octaves higher than average. Since I knew Ebony would be joining me momentarily, I dropped onto the end of the couch.

"Disney World?" I said, trying to sound surprised enough to make her believe I hadn't been in on the secret. "What are you doing there?"

"I got to meet Mickey! And Minnie!" she squealed. "And they took a picture with me!"

"They did? That's fantastic!"

"Oh, Mama, today was just the best day *ever*!"

I was happy for my baby. I mean, she was at Disney

World, every kid's dream vacation for at least the last half a century. Her joy was palpable, even over the phone. But let me be honest for a moment. When she said it was the best day *ever*, my smile dropped just a little bit. As happy as I am that Rex's parents stay involved in Anna's life and that they took her to Disney, I have to admit, I was more than a little envious. I would have loved to have been the one to take her to that magical place and see her face light up when she saw her favorite movie characters. As her only living parent, *I'm* supposed to be the one giving her the best days ever, at least until she's grown and married.

I swallowed my negative emotions and said, "I want to hear all about it. Start at the beginning."

"Well, I helped Grandmother make breakfast this morning, and then we checked to make sure I had everything in my suitcase. Then Grandfather drove us all to the airport, and when we got to the place to wait for our plane, we found Aunt Gina, Uncle Jace, and Cody waiting for us!"

I knew, of course, that the whole family was going. Gina had always been very sweet to me, and her husband and son were a delight. I continued to play along. "Really? What were they doing there?"

Anna laughed. "They came here, too!"

"Oh, how fun!"

"They have their own room, though. I'm staying in a room with Grandmother and Grandfather. I get to sleep on my own bed, and it folds up and *rolls*!"

"Oh, cool."

"But we were all on the same plane together. I got to sit next to the window, and I looked out to see if I could see our house, but I couldn't because we were too high up, like when we go to Uncle Hunter's. I don't know how far it is to here, but Grandfather said we're visiting the sunshiny state, and that they grow oranges here, but we haven't seen any."

"Well, they probably don't grow oranges at Disneyland," I offered.

"This is Disney *World*, Mama. Disneyland is somewhere else. I don't think they grow oranges there, either."

My daughter, always making sure I don't make a mistake.

"So, what did you see when you got there?"

"Oh, it was so cool! We saw Cinderella's castle! It's so pretty! And at night, when the sun is gone, it turns PINK! And then they shoot fireworks!"

"Fireworks? In March? That's amazing!" I tried my best to sound suitably amazed . . . and if I didn't quite succeed, Anna was too excited to notice. "That's a lot to see in one day."

"Oh, that isn't everything. We rode on Dumbo! It was really kind of like one of the rides at the fair, but all the seats had a Dumbo, and we went up in the air like we were flying. We went to see where Aladdin lives, and we rode on a carousel that had all these pretty horses on it. The horses were way prettier than the ones at the fair. Then we rode on a big boat that took us past all these animals. And we went on *two* trains! One was kind of scary because it around a huge mountain and it was all shaky like it might break, but Grandfather said it was supposed to feel like that because they wanted us to feel like we were on a train from the olden days. And the other train—it wasn't as bumpy—it took us to see all the dwarfs."

Her excitement was contagious. My genuine grin had returned, and I had only half a thought toward correcting the usage of "dwarfs."

"Did you get to meet any of them?"

"We didn't get to on the train, because some of them were doing stuff, and we didn't after the train because there were a lot of people and they were really busy taking pictures. Also, we had to go to the castle after that, so we didn't wait around."

"Oh, I'm sorry, baby."

"No! The castle was so cool! Grandmother took me to a beauty store called Bippity, Boppity, Booooootique, and they made me look just like a princess!"

"You went *where*?"

Anna repeated the name of the salon, drawing out the "Boo" in boutique even longer than the first time.

"I got to have my picture taken with a real prince!"

"You did? What was his name?"

"*Charming*, Mama," she said emphatically. "Only Prince Charming lives at the castle with Cinderella."

I could easily picture Anna's eyes rolling around in her head. I stifled a giggle and said, "Oh, of course. Silly me."

"That's okay. Grandfather took them with a camera that wasn't on his phone, but he said he'd send them to you." Anna paused long enough to yawn, the day's excitement finally getting to her. "What did you do today, Mama?"

"I did what I usually do on Sundays. I went to church, then went to Aunt Win's. When I came home, I worked in the garden for a little while. Nothing too exciting." I honestly didn't think being questioned by the police fell into the "exciting" category, and I didn't want to taint Anna's vacation with ideas that I might be in trouble, so I left out that little detail. "How long do you think you'll be at Disneyland . . . um, World?"

"I don't know. Grandmother won't tell me. But that's why she didn't want me to unpack my suitcase yesterday. She didn't want us to leave anything at home that we might need."

"Of course." I swallowed another chuckle. "That makes sense. She loves you too much to want you to go home after only one day."

"Uh-huh." Anna yawned again. "Did you think about my homework today?"

"I did," I said slowly, surprised that after all the excitement my daughter still had homework on her mind.

"Oh, goody!" she exclaimed with a fair amount of enthusiasm. "What will my verse be?"

"Well, I had a lot of trouble making up my mind . . ." On the other end of the line, I heard my daughter sigh heavily, possibly in defeat. "I narrowed it down to three verses, and I'm going to read them to you and let you decide."

"Okay! What's first?"

I couldn't contain my laugh. "I haven't written them down yet, and it's getting late, so we'll start tomorrow night."

"Okay." Her lackluster reply could have been from thinking I'd let her down or possibly because she was tired. It was hard to tell without looking at her face. She immediately perked back up. "Does that mean we'll be here for three more days?!"

"Maybe." I intended to tease her along a little, but

she interrupted me before I could say any more.

"Oh, yay!" She was silent for a moment while she performed what I could only imagine was some sort of dance of joy. In the background, I could hear Mr. Greene laughing. "Mama, I love you so much!"

I chuckled again. "I love you, too, baby girl."

"I should probably go to bed now. I'm a little tired, and I want to be ready for tomorrow. Will you listen to my prayer before we hang up?"

"Of course, sweetie. It'll be just like when you're at home."

I heard some rustling, and guessed Anna was probably getting under the covers on her roll-away bed. After some shuffling, she told her grandparents she was going to say her prayer and asked them to listen, too. When Anna came back on the line, she thanked God for the exciting day, for the family members with her, and for showing her Disney World. She continued by asking the Lord to bless those of us back home in Texas, Mickey and Minnie Mouse, and the little girl who had cried so hard after dropping her ice cream earlier in the evening. Anna finished by asking Him to say "hi" to her Daddy in heaven. By the time she said "Amen," I had tears rolling down my cheeks.

"Good night, Mama. I love you."

"I love you, too, Anna Claire. Have fun tomorrow."

"Can I call you again tomorrow night?"

"If it's all right with your grandmother and grandfather."

"Okay. I'll ask. Good night."

With everything that had happened during the day, I was bone-weary by the time I crawled into bed. (Yes, I was alone.) The call from Anna had, of course, given me a reason to be happy and relaxed. I called my inside dog, Robin, up onto the bed, snuggled into the blankets, and drifted off to sleep, too tired to worry about what Monday might have in store for me.

Chapter 11

I had an 8:30 appointment with a golden retriever Monday morning. By the time Goldie was bathed, dried, and had received her canine pedicure, I'd gotten three more appointment cancellations for the coming week and one for the following week. That meant that I had seven extra openings in my schedule, a little less than one-third of my business. This was not good. Upon returning Goldie to her human, an artistic and enthusiastic dancer named Frieda Haygood, I was treated to an interrogation on the pet abductions that would have garnered praise from those who engineered the Spanish Inquisition. The fact that I knew almost nothing didn't keep her from asking the same questions multiple times. Each answer I provided was a quality combination of both professionalism and reassurance. Once Ms. Haygood was satisfied with my responses, we scheduled Goldie's next appointment, and I headed over to take care of my ten thirty dachshund.

I was only delayed by twenty minutes or so.

There was a car in the driveway at the doxie's

house, and I could hear a television inside, but when I rang the doorbell, no one answered. I waited a few moments, knocked, and waited some more. I could hear the dog barking at me from the other side of the door, but no one came to answer. My attempt to call them from my cellphone only resulted in endless ringing. I was sure they were home, but left anyway, annoyed that they hadn't had the decency to tell me themselves.

That doorstep-ditch made cancellation number eight for the week. Now I was mad. This had to stop.

I had two and a half hours until my next appointment—assuming it held. I texted Win to see if she wanted to meet me for lunch downtown, then I drove around for a little while. A news story on the radio piqued my interest when they made mention of the recent pet thefts. I turned up the volume and listened while they interviewed Detective Swaim, who urged people to keep their pets inside or secured in a kennel. They asked him several questions about possible suspects and promising leads, but he was able to answer without going into specifics. Before the story was over, the reporter mentioned "a local dog groomer" who had been questioned and released. They hadn't mentioned me by name, but it wouldn't be hard for the locals to put two and two together and surmise it was me.

With this in mind, I gave some thought to what I was doing. Part of me said driving around looking for clues was a stupid idea. If more animals were taken in the areas where I was combing the streets, it would look bad for me. I had no reason to be there. No alibi. Then again, maybe I'd get lucky enough to see something that would help solve this puzzle or at least take the spotlight off me.

By the time my sister accepted my lunch invitation, it was almost eleven thirty, and I was tired of wasting gas looking at empty side streets. I drove over to a little café that is about two blocks from the courthouse, stationed my van in the shadow of a still-bare tree, put a flight harness on Ebony to keep him from getting away from me, and went to wait at one of the picnic tables. I'd chosen this place for lunch because it was convenient for Win and because they sold some of the best street food in town. It was called Double D Deli— and not for the reason you might think. The owners were a husband-wife team named Dave and Donna. They opened Double D the summer I moved back to Pinnacle. The menu featured a collection of wraps, paninis, and cold sandwiches made from a selection of about a dozen ingredients. Open from 10 in the morning until about 2 in the afternoon Monday through Friday, they were always busy, regardless of the weather. Aside from delicious, unique sandwiches, I eat at Double D because I like Dave and Donna. While they'd never made use of my grooming services or attended any of my obedience classes, I knew they had five rescue mutts in a variety of shapes, colors, and sizes. When seen in public, all their dogs appeared to be happy, healthy, and well behaved, so I was sure these two were great dog parents in addition to being excellent sandwich artists. It didn't hurt that they always gave Ebony a couple of sticks of fresh carrots when we stopped in for lunch.

Picnic tables were scattered across Double D Deli's shady lot. Since most people got their food to go, it wasn't hard to find a good seat. I set Ebony on the table and gave him a treat. He worked on cracking and eating peanuts while I people-watched. I didn't know many of those who walked by, but apparently several of them knew me. Pinnacle is a friendly town where people will greet you with a smile even if they don't know you—at least, that's what usually happens. Today, no one smiled at me, and very few even met my eyes. Several whispered and glanced at me over their shoulders, which again stirred my anger. *It's not me!* I wanted to scream, though I knew that would only make me stand out more. *Why would I try to steal the same animals that my job depends on?*

Anna's Spring Break assignment popped into my head while I thought about rude people and judging others. When another pair of whispering witches scurried past me, I decided to do an internet search on my phone for "Bible passages about judging others." I knew the line I was looking for, but I wanted to be sure I had the wording and reference right.

There were several entries on my Google search page that listed instances of lessons on jumping to conclusions about the actions of others. I had to scroll almost all the way down to the bottom of the first page before I found the entry I wanted. This particular listing was for the King James Bible online, and it referenced Matthew chapter 7, verse 1: "Judge not, that ye not be judged."

Those were the words that popped into my head every time someone tried to hide the fact that they were pointing at me while talking. In fact, since they were obviously judging me, I didn't feel so bad about the mean thoughts that popped into my head.

Judge not, that ye not be judged.

It was perfect. Short enough for Anna to learn quickly and straightforward enough for me to explain without a lot of effort.

Just as I finished copying the passage to the memo app on my phone, I saw Winter strolling toward me. When I see my sister anywhere in public, I always feel a rush of pride. She's smart—a rising start in the district attorney's office—and gorgeous. Taller than I am by several inches, Win has long, thick, dark hair with natural gold highlights (even *in* winter) and light-colored eyes that add an exotic, almost mystical quality to her appearance. On the other hand, I've heard that once, while cross-examining a witness in court, her gaze became so intensely frosty that the man on the witness stand confessed on the spot and later had to be sedated. Did I mention that even after birthing three kids, she has a figure that would make a swimsuit model envious? More important than her looks, my sister is brilliant and kind. Growing up, I idolized her. I wanted nothing more from life than to be Winter Gruene.

Hah! So much for that. We are nothing alike.

Win glided to a stop next to the table, tipped her sunglasses down to look over them at me, then straightened. Loud enough for everyone in the county to hear, she said, "There's my baby sister! She's the nicest person to have *ever* drawn a breath in Pinnacle, Texas!"

People turned to look while I flushed so fiercely my hair curled . . . more. Ebony drew several chuckles by hopping up and down, hollering, "Win! Win! Win!" before he flew to her shoulder.

My sister laughed, clearly enjoying the attention

and my mortification. And darn it—even her laugh was gorgeous!

I retrieved Ebony and waited at the table while she went to order our food. Every time I looked at the menu for Double D, I vowed I'd order something new on my next visit, but I never did. My go-to, absolute favorite panini is called the "Wild Dog." It's a pair of thick hot dogs, sliced down the middle, and topped with spinach, avocado, pepper jack cheese, sauerkraut, sweet relish, barbeque sauce, and spicy mustard, all squished between two slices of multigrain bread and toasted. Messy and full of flavor, it never fails to make my tummy happy.

Win was shaking her head and smiling at me when she returned with our food. Sitting down, she said, "Ivy, I swear you get into more trouble than anyone I know."

"What'd I do this time?" I asked, before biting into my warm, spicy mess of a sandwich.

"Oh, you know perfectly well that it isn't what you did, but what everyone *thinks* you did."

I nodded. "I really don't want to talk about it."

"I understand, but if you want Henry to go have a chat with our new detective about pointing fingers at you every time he gets a new case, just say the word."

I started to laugh but ended up getting choked on my food. My sister's husband, Henry Kowalski, is the sweetest and most mellow man on the planet. He's slender, balding, bespectacled, and an inch shorter than his drop-dead-gorgeous wife. The only way a word from Henry would stop anyone from doing anything would be if the recipient felt guilty for disappointing such a nice man.

After regaining my composure (again), the rest of

our lunch passed without mention of missing animals, blame, or anything in the whole spectrum of the laws of our country. Instead, Win told me about the wonders of Disney World, and we speculated on what Anna might be doing.

When we were finished, I gave my sister a ride back to the courthouse. While the walk might have helped her burn off some of the fuel she'd just consumed, she claims it isn't easy to walk downhill in heels when you're completely stuffed. As we pulled out of the Double D parking lot, I looked to my left for oncoming traffic and saw a white pickup turn in the opposite direction. White pickups are a dime a dozen in East Texas, but this one had a weathered bed topper on the back, and "Pinnacle Animal Control" was written in peeling black letters on the door.

At first, I didn't think much of it, but the more I tried to push it from my mind, the more the image insisted on remaining in the forefront. I realized I hadn't seen an animal shelter truck like that in a long time. It had been at least five years since the local pound closed its doors to be replaced by a state-of-the-art, no-kill facility. With the new facility came new vehicles, and if I remembered correctly, they were bright yellow with a paw print on each door.

I was still pondering this when my phone rang. Win climbed out of the van and waved goodbye as I answered the call from the lady who owned the dog for my next appointment. Fortunately, she was only calling to be sure I was still coming.

After leaving Win, I went directly to the home of one of the oddest-looking dogs I've ever seen—some sort of a Chihuahua mix who is always cold and only stops shivering when I turn on the blow dryer. Imagine a tan Chihuahua with long floppy ears, half a tail, and legs long enough that they looked like custom-made doggy stilts. This one also has dense fur in a narrow band down her back, with the rest of her hair becoming thinner, more delicate, and paler as it moves down to her toes, leaving the poor baby looking like her paws are bare. The dog's name is, of all things, Snookums, and like many aesthetically challenged creatures, she has a sweet disposition.

Now, you may be wondering why a small, short-haired dog such as this would need grooming services. Two reasons: one, her toenails grow faster than anything I've ever seen, and two, she has a skin condition that seems to respond positively only to my minty oatmeal shampoo. Snookums' person, Nina, *could* purchase the shampoo and bathe her dog herself, but toenail clipping is another story; after a traumatic experience when Nina insisted that her Snookums wouldn't look her in the eye after she had clipped her nails too short, she decided she would only entrust her pooch's pedicures to the experts—me.

After a nearly stress-free grooming session, I returned Snookums to her hu-mom and decided to head home. The rest of my afternoon clients had canceled, and I needed to finish hacking apart the dirt in my vegetable garden, so I decided to call it a day. Just as I was about to step into my mobile grooming salon, I saw a flash of white out of the corner of my eye. I turned to see what looked like the same white pickup, identical to the one I'd seen as we left lunch. As quickly as I could, I got behind the wheel and turned my monstrous mobile grooming salon around. It isn't easy maneuvering a rolling billboard on a side street, and by the time I was pointing the right way, the truck was long gone.

The new Pinnacle animal shelter wasn't far off my accustomed route home, so I decided to take an extra few minutes and stop in. Three sunny-yellow pickups were parked behind the building, their doors festooned with a green paw print bearing the shelter's acronym, PAWS, which stood for "Pinnacle Animal Welfare Services." The trucks themselves had built-in animal crates. A sign above the facility's door bore the same logo. What I didn't see was an everyday pickup with black lettering.

Chapter 12

Perhaps not surprisingly, I ended up spending way too much time at PAWS. It wasn't entirely my fault, though. Someone came through with a box full of kittens, and one of the furry little charmers conned me into getting on the floor to play. While down there, another of the purring rascals curled up in my lap and went to sleep, and it took all my willpower not to scoop it up and take it home.

I don't know how Ebony would react to a cat, or vice versa, but somehow I managed to convince myself that I genuinely did not need another furry companion, especially if my business was about to go down the tubes because of innuendo and gossip.

It was after four by the time I made it home. I got Ebony situated inside with a treat puzzle and changed into old clothes, with the intention of going out and getting dirty. As I retrieved my gardening rake and started for my plot of weeds, I found something unexpected: it had been plowed for me. I was contemplating this development when the phone in my pocket started mooing at me.

"Hi, this is Ivy," I answered, without looking at the caller ID.

"Ivy!" This declaration was followed by a series of sobs, and ". . . with you?"

I glanced at the screen to see it was Becky Hopkins, the owner of a loveable—if stubborn—bloodhound. Bentley is one of my favorite clients.

"Wait, say that again?"

"Bentley . . ." She sobbed again. "He's not here! I just came home. Is he with you?"

It felt like someone had poured frigid water on my soul. "Becky, you need to breathe. Take a big deep breath, hold it for a sec, and let it back out." I listened as she did as I instructed. "What makes you think Bentley isn't at home?"

"He's always waiting for me at the door when I walk in, and today he wasn't. I looked outside, and I called him, but he's not here."

"Okay, you need to call the police. Now."

"What?"

"Hang up and dial 9-1-1. I'll be there as soon as I can."

I peeled out of my driveway so fast that I think I left some of Rex's bright red pickup paint in the driveway. On the way to Becky's, I caught every red light and got behind every slowpoke in the eastern third of the state. A trip that should have taken me fifteen minutes felt like hours, but eventually I skidded to a stop in front of Becky's house. I was just getting out of the pickup when Detective Swaim brought his unmarked car in for a landing right behind me. I didn't have time to worry about the fact that it looked like he was pulling me over (yet again). I ran to the door and knocked.

Swaim and I were ushered in by an extremely courteous and calm Pinnacle police officer named Dennis March. I've known Dennis since kindergarten, and he was probably the best person to have responded to Becky's call. He led the way to where Becky sat on her couch, blubbering into a kitchen towel. I sat down next to her while Swaim perched on a nearby chair. When prompted by the detective, she explained the steps she'd taken upon entering the house and finding it Bentley-less. While she spoke, Dennis wandered off to points unknown, only to return with an odd look on his face. He waved to Swaim, and the two men disappeared for a few moments.

Over the next thirty minutes or so, it became apparent that someone had broken into Becky's house through a side door and had spirited Bentley out and away. By the time a crime scene investigator had arrived to dust for prints, Becky's husband had come home, and the two of them huddled together like shipwreck survivors adrift on the ocean. I felt terrible for them and utterly helpless. Of course, those feelings evaporated as soon as Swaim pulled me aside.

"Ms. Greene, I need to know where you were today," he said, after ushering me into another room.

"You think *I* did this? Are you crazy? I *like* these people. They're nice, and they're some of my best customers. Why would I take their dog?"

"Ivy, please, I need to do my job. Just tell me where you've been all day. I just need the names and numbers of the clients you saw today."

The detective actually looked pained by his questions, but I refused to feel bad for him. Instead, I pulled out my phone and gave him the information on the two clients I'd actually seen and the one I was sure had been home but had failed to answer the door. When I finished, he shook his head, obviously disappointed.

"So you didn't work between ten and one, or after two?"

I shook my head. "I was over at PAWS for a while this afternoon. I went there after Nina Barrett's house. After that, I went home to work in my yard."

"What is PAWS?"

"It's the animal shelter."

"Is your schedule usually this light? Or is it because of Spring Break at the college?"

"No," I answered indignantly. "Everyone in town knows you questioned me yesterday about the missing pets, and half my customers are afraid to let me near their babies for fear I'll run off with them. So, it's basically *your* fault my schedule has gaping holes in it."

Swaim shook his head again but didn't apologize or even look particularly fazed by my response. Instead, he asked, "What were you doing at the shelter?"

I suddenly realized that in all the excitement over Bentley, I'd forgotten about the white pickup. I began to explain about lunch with Win and the white pickup I'd seen that seemed out of place. Swaim nodded and made notes while I talked. When I mentioned that my idea of following the pickup had been foiled by my van's horrible turn radius, he stopped writing and nailed me with an angry glare.

"Tell me you aren't serious," he said.

"Of course, I'm serious. My van is way too big to make sharp turns, especially on a side street."

"That's not what I meant. I was hoping you were going to tell me you weren't going to do any snooping on your own."

I shrugged. "That's why I went over to PAWS. I wanted to see what kind of trucks they drive."

"And?"

"And I hung around to play with a bunch of kittens." I knew that wasn't what he was asking, but I wanted to irritate him just a little to make up for his accusations. It wasn't much, but it's all I had. He rewarded my efforts with a growl that came from a tightly clenched jaw.

"What kind of trucks do they drive?" he asked, saying each word carefully.

"They're not white, if that's what you mean."

The detective flipped his notebook closed and looked at the ceiling. I'm not a lip-reader, but I'm sure I saw him silently counting to ten. "Go home, Ivy. Go do whatever you were going to do and please stay away from this investigation."

"*Your* investigation? *She* called *me*. I'm the one who told her to call 9-1-1. It's *because* of me that you're even here right now." I could feel my anger feeding itself. "And if you think about it, you're the whole reason I'm involved anyway!"

"How—" he started.

"Don't interrupt me," I scolded, pointing my finger at him. On some deep, subconscious level, I could see that Luke was losing control of his temper. It didn't matter. I was full of resentment and I was going to spew it all over him. Just like a runaway freight train, there was no stopping me now. "You started your investigation with me because I was the easy target. You listened to baseless rumors and jumped into the middle of my personal business, hoping to score a quick win and make yourself look like a genius. It's *your* fault that customers have started canceling on me. If—and that's a really big 'if'—I'm poking around in this problem, it's totally out of self-defense. I have to clear my name or lose my livelihood. You aren't from a small town, so you don't know what it's like to have people continually watching you and judging you. Reputation is ninety-five percent of my success, and if I can't find a way to clear myself of suspicion, no one is going to do it for me, so *don't* tell me to stay out of it."

Luke waited a beat before speaking. I'd like to think it was because he was interested in what I had to say, but it's more likely he just wanted to see if I was out of gas. Sadly, I was.

"I'm sorry if I've put you in a tough spot," he started. When I opened my mouth to protest, he held up one hand. "Let me finish. I know how small towns work. You and I both know that your clients started canceling on you as soon as they saw us talking the other day, and that had nothing to do with an investigation. We were talking, and someone jumped to the wrong conclusion. I started my investigation with you so I could maybe stop those rumors and clear the noise around you. I was trying to help, not put you out of business. You driving around in places where you don't belong is just going to make people more suspicious, and the more attention you draw, the harder it is for me to focus my energy on the real perpetrators."

I drew in a deep breath while I thought about what he was saying. I knew he was right about when the gossiping had begun, but I didn't want to admit it. I also didn't want to let go of my anger.

I narrowed my eyes and shook my finger at him

again. There were thousands . . . well, maybe hundreds, or at least tens, of things I wanted to say at that moment, but I didn't. Instead, I straightened my shoulders, turned on my heel, and left.

Chapter 13

When I answered my phone Monday night, I was greeted by a drawn-out yodel in Anna's voice.

"Do you know who that was?" She asked once she had her giggles under control. Without waiting for me to answer, she said, "Granddaddy said there used to be a jungle king who would sound like that. His name was Tarzan. Do you know who that is? I've been practicing, but I don't sound much like Granddaddy when he does it. Guess what we did today!"

It occurred to me that Anna had just called Mr. Greene 'Grandaddy' not once, but twice. Instead of mentioning it, I said, "I—"

"We went on a safari! It was just like going to Africa, only we're still in Disney World. We got on this big bus that didn't have walls so we could see the animals. We saw real zebras and giraffes! Oh, Mama, they are so pretty in real life when they're out moving around. You know, giraffes walk around like princesses. They just glide along and look at everybody. Do you think all giraffes are girls?"

I had to wait a moment to be sure it was actually my

turn to talk. "No, baby, I think to have giraffes, some of them have to be boys."

"Hmm . . . okay. Anyway, we saw rhinoceroses, too! And real live lions kind of like at the zoo, but better because these weren't in cages! And at the end of the safari, we saw these *huge* dirt piles that are supposed to be where termites live! I'm glad we don't have termites at home, because their houses would take up too much of our yard. You wouldn't be able to run the mower over them, even!"

"Seriously? You know I can run the mower over just about anything." This is true. I try to pick up the things in my yard before I mow, but there always seems to be something that gets shredded—trash, dog toys, maybe a random shoe. Anna has also watched as I've run over fire ant mounds.

"These things are almost as big as your purple truck!"

"Wow, that *is* big. How big are the termites?"

"I don't know. We didn't see any of them. We just saw their hills. We went somewhere else to look at bugs."

"You went to look at bugs? On your safari?"

Anna laughed. "No, silly."

While my baby girl babbled on about the sights and sounds of her day, my mind insensitively wandered off in the direction of dogs—namely stolen dogs. I was still trying to figure out what kind of money could be made in snatching someone else's dog. To show a dog on a professional circuit, you would need documentation from the American Kennel Club to prove that the dog you're showing is purebred. To breed dogs and sell them for profit, you again need proof of bloodlines. I supposed that there was sponsorship money to be made in agility and other competitions for dogs of undocumented breeding, but it seemed like there would be much easier ways to make money than stealing a dog that still had to be trained.

". . . and we saw a movie about how hard it is to be a bug."

I tuned into Anna just in time to be confused.

"It's hard to be a bug?"

"Oh, they think so. Because people are always trying to slap them and step on them and spray them with poison. They have to work really hard to stay alive."

"I guess I never thought of it that way."

"I didn't either. The movie was funny, but it didn't make me like bugs. I mean, *those* bugs were better than what we have at home because they talked and stuff, but they weren't real."

"So, next time we see a bug in the bathtub, do you want to try to save it?"

"No!"

Anna's response was so emphatic that I had to laugh. "So you went on a safari and to a big tree today. Is that all you did?"

"Oh, we also went on a walk in a forest where gorillas live!"

"Gorillas?" My mouth said the word, but my brain ricocheted off into my mental wilderness.

Where would you keep multiple dogs that weren't yours? A single dog would be easy enough to conceal and explain, but once you get multiple dogs in an unfamiliar environment without the security of their owners, they're going to make noise—a *lot* of noise.

And having several new dogs suddenly appear in your backyard is going to raise eyebrows . . . and questions.

I realized Anna had gone quiet. In an effort to make it seem like I'd been listening, I referenced the last subject I could remember. "Were there bugs in their forest?"

"No, but it was super hot. It was when we got done, so it could just be hot here, and not just because of the gorilla place."

"You're probably right. It was a little warm here today, too, and as far as I know, we don't have any gorillas in the woods."

Anna giggled at me again. "You're so silly, Mama. Oh, and guess what! When we left the gorillas, we went on another boat ride. This one was so cool because—actually, it really *was* cool, because it wasn't hot in there, but also we went through this cave, and . . ."

My disobedient brain focused on caves. Do we have caves in East Texas? I couldn't remember any offhand, but that didn't mean there wasn't a hollow structure somewhere out in the woods.

Before figuring out the *where* I needed to unravel the *why*. Why would someone risk being arrested for breaking and entering just to steal a dog?

Outside, Baskin barked, then growled, snarled, and barked again. I experienced a momentary flashback to the night several months ago when a man broke into my house. Baskin barked that night, too, but his attempt to protect me then had led him to get too close to the intruder and earned him a solid kick in the chest. That night, my little dog yelped and ran for cover. Since then, he's much faster and doesn't usually get close to humans he doesn't know. Since his current ruckus didn't seem to have changed location, I felt confident that whatever animal he was battling had decided to fight back. I would need to check him for wounds before I went to bed.

Then it hit me: Dog Fighting.

I remembered a book I'd read in school about a dog in the 1800s that was stolen from his posh home and taken to another state to be used in fighting, simply because he was a big dog. These days, people still train dogs for fighting in spite (or maybe because) of the fact that it's illegal. I couldn't remember just how illegal, but the fact that a major sports star served prison time for it had stuck in my head. There are always horror stories circulating about people who claim free dogs and use them for training the actual fighters.

Not all dogs like confrontation and most have to be taught to fight—either by their canine parents or the people who own them. Bentley is a big, sweet baby of a dog that weighs around a hundred pounds. He does not have a mean bone in his body. A chill ran down my spine, horrible images of beaten and bloodied dogs flashed through my mind, and dread filled my stomach to the point that I was afraid I might get sick. I took a deep breath and tuned in to the sweet voice that was chattering away on the other end of the line.

". . . Aunt Gina said it was a movie. They have mountains there that just hang in the air and plants that light up all on their own without lights. The people who live there are blue."

"Blue? You mean like a Smurf?"

"No, these people are taller and a different color of blue."

"Oh, okay." I was getting frighteningly good at

playing dumb. "What else did you do today?"

"Mama! Don't you think that was enough?"

I could hear the Greenes chuckling in the background. "Well, sure, it sounds like plenty to me, but I wasn't there."

"It was really fun, all of it. It was so cool to see animals running around free."

"I'll bet it was."

"Did you do anything today? I mean, anything but work?"

I didn't even consider telling her the whole truth. Anna didn't need to know about Bentley or my ever-increasing worries.

"No, that's pretty much all I did. I had lunch with Aunt Win. And I stopped off at PAWS and played with some baby kitties."

Anna gasped. "Kitties! Did you bring me one home? Is it cute? What color is it?"

Lord, I am such an idiot.

"No, baby, I didn't bring a kitten home. I don't know if Ebony would be safe with a kitten."

"We could teach it to be nice to Ebony."

The pleading in her voice, combined with the memory of that little fuzz ball purring in my ear while it slept, was almost enough to break my resolve. Almost, but not quite.

"Ebony isn't the only one we'd have to worry about. You know how Baskin is about other animals in the yard. He might not realize the kitten was ours and hurt it."

"Oh, yeah." All the happiness left Anna's voice, leaving the night darker than it had been before.

"I'm sorry I mentioned it, baby," I mumbled.

"It's okay, Mama." She paused a beat before picking up a little verbal momentum. "Did you remember to write down the Bible stuff for me?"

"I did." Sometimes it pays to have extra time on your hands, regardless of the reason. "Do you want to hear the first one?"

"Yes, please!"

I put my phone on speaker mode and went to the app where I'd made notes for Anna's project. I'd narrowed down the passage choices to three and experienced a moment of panic while I tried to decide on which one to read first. Finally, I decided to just go with the words written next to the number "1." "Okay, tonight's verse is from the book of Hebrews. It says, 'Now, faith is confidence in what we hope for and assurance for what we do not see.'"

Anna repeated a few words, then said the rest with me as I reread them. Then she asked, "What does that mean?"

"It means that when we believe in God—when we have faith—we can count on Him to keep His promises even though we can't see Him the way we see people or things around us."

"Oh." In that one word, Anna conveyed her confusion.

"It's just something for you to think about. Can you see God the same way you can see me?"

"I can't see you right now."

"No, but you can hear my voice. If you were here, you'd be able to look at me, right?"

"Yes, ma'am. So, it's like I have faith that you are at home, just like I believe God and Daddy are in heaven?"

"Yes." I wanted to give her time to make more connections, but I was afraid I might have chosen a verse that was too abstract.

"And when you make me a promise, it's like the promises God makes to us?"

"Yes, in a way. When I make you a promise, do you see it immediately?"

She went quiet, then muttered a soft "hmm" before answering. "Sometimes, but not very often."

"If you don't see it right away, how do you know I'll keep my promise?"

"Because you always try, Mama."

"Right."

Anna asked me to read her the verse again. "I'll try to think about it tomorrow. Right now, I'm kind of tired, and I don't know if my head wants to work that hard."

I had to laugh. "I understand completely, baby girl. And if you decide you don't like this verse, I have two more you can try."

"Okay" She sounded relieved. "Will you listen to my prayers again tonight, before we hang up?"

"You know I will."

Again, there was a lot of shuffling, followed by Anna's request that the others in the room listen as well. When the background chatter ceased, she thanked God for the many animals on the planet—even the bugs we don't like—for the people who feed all the animals, and for the really yummy dessert she'd had after supper. Next, she asked Him to bless everyone at home, everyone with her in Florida, and all the animals that don't have someone to feed them. Finally, she thanked God for making sure she wasn't born a funny color like bright orange or neon green and asked that He help any of the blue people who wanted to look normal.

Chapter 14

The wind picked up Monday night, and by Tuesday morning heavy clouds had camped out over Pinnacle, with thunder rumbling in the distance. My first appointment was with an all-black standard poodle named Horatio. This dog was so laid back that working with him was like maneuvering a warm, hairy mannequin. Even the increasingly loud rumbles of thunder from the approaching storm didn't faze him.

A weather warning was coming over the radio when I stepped back into my van. The local meteorologist claimed we were only looking at a severe thunderstorm, but I had my doubts that we'd get off that easily. My mobile salon is constructed inside what most people would consider a high-profile vehicle—a retired package delivery van. In other words, if not for the engine block, my rolling billboard would have become a box kite in a good stiff wind. I had about forty-five minutes before my next scheduled appointment—not long enough to drive home and wait out the storm, but too long to sit out in the open, exposed to the elements. The rain started as I turned onto the main road, and by the time I'd driven only a few blocks, the downpour increased until visibility was dangerously inhibited.

From what I could tell, the wind was now coming from a westerly direction, so I decided to seek shelter behind a strip mall. This wouldn't get me out of the rain, but I was hoping that by parking close to the back of the building, I'd be spared some of the flying objects that the wind might hurl in my direction. By the time I found a suitable space, the sky was beginning to turn a funky green.

Once parked, I tried to sit in Anna's seat but soon hopped back up. I'm not good at waiting, and the highly charged air was making it impossible for me to sit still. I patted myself on the back for leaving Ebony at home and started making sure the tools stored above my workstation were adequately secured.

A brief lull in the heavy rain afforded me the sight of a guy walking along the side of the building in my direction, his head down and arms folded tightly across his chest in a futile effort to stave off the chill of the storm. I'd parked close enough to the wall that he was going to have to leave the meager protection of the structure and walk around my van. I moved up to the windshield and knocked on it, drawing the walker's attention. Waving at him, I motioned toward the driver's door. As he broke into a trot, I took a moment to ponder my invitation. I was about to offer shelter to a stranger, and it occurred to me that this was probably not the smartest move I'd ever made. It was, however, a little late to back out. Just as this thought popped into my head, tiny balls of ice began to drop from the sky. I flipped up the driver's seat and pulled open the door, flattening myself against the divider so the poor, soaking wanderer could get in out of the weather.

SUSAN BYRDE

"Thank you," exclaimed the guy who was now dripping on my floorboards.

He was younger than I am by a few years, with dark hair and brown eyes. I invited him to sit in Anna's seat while I went to get a towel or two.

"You picked some pretty nasty weather to take a walk," I said, as I eased up onto the counter to sit next to the sink.

The guy chuckled. "Yeah, I just got off work. I thought I'd get home before the bottom fell out of the cloud. I guess this is what I get for thinking!"

I smiled and nodded, looking toward the windshield at the curtains of rain. Small hailstones beat a steady rhythm on the roof above our heads.

"I'm Daryl."

"Ivy," I said, shaking the slippery hand he offered before passing him a towel.

"I came here from Arizona," he said, as he began to dry his pant legs. "We don't usually get weather like this at home."

I nodded. "This is pretty typical for springtime here. What brought you to Pinnacle?"

He shrugged. "I got it in my head to see some of the country before I get too old, so I hopped on a bus. I went to California first and just started making my way east. I was almost out of money, so I decided to stop here and work a little bit before moving on."

My head bobbed up and down while I tried to think of something else to say. Daryl had gotten as much water off his clothes as he was able and now turned his attention to the puddles on the floor. As he reached to mop up the water at his feet, I saw a flash of green on his back just above the collar of his shirt. It was a bright

106

stripe of smudged color.

Before I realized I was going to speak, I blurted, "Oh, I know who you are!"

"Huh?" Daryl sat up, holding the towel between his hands.

"You're the leprechaun." Even as the words tumbled out of my mouth, I wondered why I couldn't just shut up. The motor that drove my mouth continued to spew my unfiltered thoughts. "I saw you last week. Friday morning, I think it was."

"Really?" he squeaked.

"Yeah, you ran past me after I finished with a dog the other day. We were over on Walnut."

"What makes you think it was me?" he asked in a guarded tone.

Part of my brain begged my lips to seal shut, while another part began to wonder what I'd done with my phone.

"You have green paint at the base of your neck."

Daryl reached back and wiped the spot with the very damp towel in his hands. It came away with the remnants of his paint-on costume. He sounded disappointed when he said, "Oh."

I patted my pockets and found my phone.

"Are you going to turn me in?"

My search came to a screeching halt as unbidden memories popped into my head of the last time I got involved in someone else's crime. Achy head, bruises, being choked unconscious, hiding in a closet with my pistol . . . It was all related to that incident with the dead body and I really didn't want a repeat of any of those actions.

"Umm . . ."

"Please don't," he begged. "I'm not hurting anybody."

The word "hurting" made me wonder if I needed to start carrying a gun while I worked.

"How do you know?" I asked. "What makes you think you aren't traumatizing someone's poor kid or giving someone nightmares?"

Daryl surprised us both by laughing. "Why would a dancing leprechaun give someone nightmares?"

"I don't know," I admitted. A mental picture of Anna popped in my head. "What if someone's little girl saw you?"

"I'm really careful to only dance during the day when kids are at school, and I try to go to places where there will be little old ladies."

"Why?"

"Well, they seem to really enjoy watching me. They always clap and have such a good time. Besides, if they get mad, I can usually outrun them."

It occurred to me that he wasn't quite grasping the problem with running around flashing people. I wondered if he was being dense on purpose, like I'd done with Detective Swaim.

"What made you start . . . *dancing*?"

"I got started when I was in Los Angeles. I got a job as a sanitation technician for a company that sends strippers out for birthday parties and bridal showers. At first, they wouldn't hire me as a dancer. They said I didn't have the right body type, which just meant that I needed to work out and get fit. Then this one day in January, a guy called in sick, and I was the only one available to fill in. I really liked it, which surprised me because I'm usually shy, but getting dressed up made me feel like someone else. I was making people happy and having a lot of fun doing it. The fact that I got to make money at the same time was just a bonus. I only got to dance—professionally—that one time, but I really missed it."

I know I'm not always the sharpest tack in the box, but I was still coming to grips with the fact that he'd actually said "sanitation technician" when I realized he'd stopped talking. Finally, I asked, "How did you come up with the leprechaun thing?"

"I got the idea to freelance when I was in Oklahoma City right before Valentine's Day. I still had the pants because, you know, I had to buy my own. They're specially designed tear-away pants, and they're expensive, so I had to find something else to do with them. I decided I would dress up as Cupid. I found a red shirt and made some wings out of tissue paper. They were really kind of a pain. I had to make new ones every time it rained, and one time I almost got arrested because my wings got tangled up in a bush. After that, I had to leave town. That's when I came here.

"I told myself I needed to stop dancing if it was going to get me in trouble. I have enough of a hard time getting a job without a record, and if I get busted, well . . . Anyway, I wasn't going to do it anymore, but then here comes St. Patrick's Day and I thought, why not? It's a new town and all, and I'm getting a lot of use out of my pants."

Suddenly worried that he might jump up and demonstrate the tear-away feature, I glanced down to see if he was wearing his dancing pants. I breathed a huge sigh of relief when I saw he had on blue jeans.

"I had a green shirt, but it shrunk in the wash, so I

started using some grease paint I found on sale in a party store. I got the mask there, too."

Outside, the hail stopped, but the wind kept howling. My brain was desperately trying to grasp the absurdity of the reality I was in: sitting in my van with a flasher who called himself a dancer while a tornado was probably passing somewhere close by.

"Hmm . . ." I said, hoping to buy myself some time before he started talking again. "Where do you work now?"

"I work the night shift over at . . ." Daryl paused, his guarded look returning. "Hey, I can't tell you that. You'll tell them and get me fired. Or arrested."

"So, you *do* have an actual job that requires you to wear clothes?"

He giggled. "Oh yeah. Does this mean you're not going to out me?"

"I don't know yet." I could just see myself going to the police station and telling them that I'd given shelter to an exotic dancer who liked to strip for the elderly. I'm pretty sure someone would have me committed if I tried to explain it all.

"What if I made it worth your while?"

I made a face. The last thing I needed right now was some guy waving his personal equipment around in my van.

Daryl looked stricken. "That's not what I meant!"

I knew I couldn't take money from him. I didn't know if it was illegal to bribe a private citizen, but if I accepted money from him, it would be that much longer before he would be able to catch a bus to some other town. "What *did* you mean?"

"I've seen your camper around town. I know who

you are, kind of. You do mobile pet grooming." He motioned toward the sink at my right.

I nodded slowly, increasingly afraid of what he might have in mind.

"Well, I hear people talking, and I heard someone say that you have been stealing pets from people."

"Why would I do that?" I asked abruptly. Apparently, my vocal motor had switched on again.

He shrugged knowingly. "To resell them to labs that do animal testing."

"What?!" Angry, I jumped off the counter to stand over him.

"Hey, I didn't say that's what I thought. I'm just telling you what I've heard." He paused, probably to see if I was going to hit him with something in my anger, then leaned back in the seat as far as he could. "I'm really sure those people are all wrong. I mean, the kind of person that would let a total stranger sit in their camper during a storm isn't the kind of person who would sell animals to a drug lab."

I don't exactly drive a camper, but it was hard to fault his reasoning, even if it was a little twisted. I took half a step back and motioned for him to keep talking.

"I know stuff about the people who are really stealing the animals. I know what kind of car they drive."

"I've already figured that out, too," I said, narrowing my eyes at him in hopes of appearing menacing. "What else have you got?"

"What if I could tell you where they park when they aren't driving around picking up animals?"

I thought about this for a minute. If I could find the place where they stored their vehicle, I could follow them and take pictures of them stealing the next dog and report it to the police. Or better yet, they might even lead me to where they're keeping the pets.

"I saw this place one day when I was out running. I do that to stay in shape for dancing, you know? Anyway, I don't know the names of all the roads, but I can draw you a map," Daryl offered.

I nodded and turned to fish a notebook out of a drawer.

Taking the paper from my hand, he said, "Before I draw anything, you have to promise me you won't turn me in for my dancing."

That wasn't even a question in my mind. As far as I was concerned, family pets were a lot more important than some guy who liked to dress up like a leprechaun. Besides, tomorrow was St. Patrick's Day. How much longer could he keep dancing? Still, I didn't want to give in too quickly.

"How do I know you won't decide to dress up like the Easter Bunny and flash a bunch of schoolgirls?"

"I wouldn't . . . That's a great idea! I hadn't thought about the Easter Bunny!"

Darn my stupid mouth!

I narrowed my eyes at him again. "You have to promise me that you'll stop your *dancing* before someone gets hurt."

Daryl slouched like someone had let the air out of his balloon. Then, in the blink of an eye, he perked right up again. "What if I promise to leave Pinnacle and do my dancing somewhere else?"

I hesitated before nodding.

"Okay, I'll be on a bus to another town before the end of the week." He turned his attention to the paper in his hands and quickly drew a map to a building down a county road. When he began to label the streets, I had a pretty good idea of where I would be looking for the dog-nappers. Map completed, Daryl handed me the notebook and said hastily, "I can't promise I won't dance tomorrow, because, well, tomorrow is my big day. But I will leave after that."

As I studied the hand-drawn map, Daryl took the opportunity to jump up and run out before I could change my mind. I sighed, watching the now fully clothed streaker disappear into the easing rain. I wondered how long it would take him to apply a fresh coat of green body paint, and how it could possibly be worth it.

Chapter 15

Once it seemed that the worst of the weather had passed, I headed to my next appointment—a little Pekinese mix named Mitzi who likes to nip at me if I fail to pay her the proper attention. She was actually the perfect distraction if I was going to put my newly gained information on the back burner for a little while. I tried to put Daryl's report out of my mind. I even tried shoving the map into a drawer, but that didn't really help. Every few minutes my eyes would travel to that area, and I'd have to mentally shout at myself to keep from pulling it open and looking at the drawing again.

I felt like I knew the area Daryl had been describing. There was an old covered arena out in that direction, the site of a now-defunct livestock auction. On the surface, that would be an excellent place to hold several animals, as it was relatively isolated and had easy access for hauling things in and out. Whatever animals were being kept there could make as much noise as they wanted, and no one would be the wiser. On the other hand, the arena had pipe rail fencing and a set of old wooden bleachers on one end. With no walls or foliage to camouflage the main pen, surely anyone driving by would be able to see whatever was kept in the fenced area if they slowed down enough. However, I'm pretty sure the majority of the traffic on that road were chicken-haulers, over-familiar with the route and not on the lookout for anything unusual.

I really needed to check the validity of the map, but one of my biggest problems was that I would be driving down a rutted—if it was paved at all—backroad in a large purple box. Sure, I *could* claim to be lost if anyone asked, but the more likely scenario would be that someone would see me headed that way, suddenly remember hearing a dog somewhere out in the thicket, and turn me in, forcing me to have to explain myself yet again to Detective Swaim before I had any solid information to share with him. What I needed was a different vehicle, one that was much more inconspicuous than my own. I could probably borrow either Mama's or Daddy's car, but then I'd have to explain what I was doing or come up with a believable lie. On top of everything else, I really hate lying to people. I'm not good at it, and I always feel so guilty. On the other hand, I *could* call Detective Swaim and offer him the map; however, I could only imagine what choice words The Swami would have for me if he were to find out I was putting my amateur sleuth skills to the test. Did I really want to risk it? Would he really believe that a leprechaun had drawn me a map of the probable whereabouts of the pet thief? Not likely.

Mitzi only got her tiny little teeth on me four or five times before I pulled my mind away from the densely wooded county road that I would have to investigate later. Once she was bathed, dried, fluffed, and had a bow installed in her pretty little topknot, I returned her to her doting human. During the hand-off, Mitzi's owner asked if I'd been caught in the hailstorm earlier. While answering, an idea popped into my mind. I needed to check the roof of my van for hail damage, which would require a step ladder tall enough for me to take a peek at the top side of my work area. The closest place that would have both a ladder and a possible loaner vehicle was James' garage. He would ask questions, too, but he was less likely to grill me about the details than one of my parents.

After scheduling Mitzi's next appointment, I cranked up my van and made my way down the main road through town to the mechanic's shop that used to belong to a man named Boomer. The place had always been called Boomer's Garage, and I don't think I'd ever heard anyone refer to the original owner by a name other than Boomer. When James bought the place and reopened it, he'd changed it to Pinnacle Automotive, but for anyone who has lived here for more than ten years, it's still referred to as Boomer's Garage.

I rolled into the lot and parked as far out of the way as I could. It didn't look like James had an overwhelming amount of business, with the college kids home for a few days, but I didn't want my mobile monstrosity blocking any access points. A quick glance toward the office told me no one was in there, so I pointed my feet toward an open bay door and a pair of legs that could be seen under a sedan that was up on a large hydraulic lift.

I can never reliably predict my reactions to James. Sometimes, I feel like a normal person around him. I can carry on a reasonably intelligent conversation and never give a second thought to how I look, sound, or behave while we're together. The previous Sunday evening was a perfect example of a time when I was a sensible human adult in the company of my neighbor. We talked—well, really, *I* talked—and laughed, and we had nice time together. Other times, some seemingly insignificant factor will trigger something inside me, causing my brain to slide out of my ear and my tongue to tie itself into knots. There was no way to know ahead of time what I might see or smell or pick up with some other sense that would render me two IQ points above an amoeba. I promise, if there was something—ANYTHING—that made sense, I'd prepare myself so as to avoid looking like an idiot, but my reactions are so random there is no way to know which Ivy will present herself.

I didn't worry over much about this as I wandered into the greater garage area. There didn't appear to be anyone else around, and I had no way of knowing if James even knew I was there. I was more concerned with the map burning a hole in my pocket and whether or not my sudden presence would make the guy under the car scald himself or hit his head. I tapped on the side of the car as I approached, then announced myself.

"Howdy, neighbor!"

My words came out really loud and heavily accented, sounding more like "Haddy naaayburr" than the casual greeting that was meant. Apparently, Idiot Ivy was in charge of my vocalizations.

James peeked at me from under the car. He had one eyebrow cocked and something very close to a snarl on his lips. "Really, Ivy? Are you practicing for the lead in *The Beverly Hillbillies*?"

I giggled, further embarrassing myself. I cleared my throat, tried to regain some of my composure, and shoved my hands into my back pockets to keep from fidgeting. "Do you have a ladder? I need to see if I got any hail damage this morning."

Keeping his face utterly blank, he pointed over my shoulder to a tall stepladder leaning against the outside of the building . . . about five feet from where I'd parked. "You know if you fall, I'll laugh before I help you up."

I nodded but didn't respond with words, for fear of humiliating myself even more.

I managed to get the ladder set up, then climbed up *and* down without incident. Not only was I in one piece, but there weren't any new dents in the roof of my truck. Proud of myself, I went back to the sedan only to find that James was no longer in the garage. A quick glance around found him in the office, sitting on top of his desk, drinking a bottle of water. I went to join him, hoping I'd left Idiot Ivy behind me.

"Well?" he asked, as I walked in.

"All good," I answered, sounding almost normal. Then, before I lost my nerve, I said, "Do you have a car I can borrow real quick? I have an errand I need to run, and everything would go a lot faster if I don't have to drive my van."

He looked at me, his eyes (which looked more blue than green today) boring into me. "What kind of errand?"

"Umm, you know . . . just an errand."

Holding out a folded piece of paper, he said, "It wouldn't have anything to do with *this*, would it?"

I glanced down and saw that James was holding the

map Daryl had drawn for me. The wannabe dancer had written "DOGS?" in block letters across the top. The paper had been in my back pocket when I climbed out of my van. I stifled a groan.

"Maybe."

"Then, no, I don't have a car you can borrow." James walked around behind the desk and dropped into the chair.

"No problem," I said, trying to sound casual. "I don't really have time right now anyway."

I started to reach for the map, only to have James pull it away.

"What was your plan here, Ivy? Were you going to drive out to . . ." he looked down at the lines on the page, "County Road 515? Maybe creep around and see if you can find some lost dogs and clear your name?"

I shrugged and stuck my hands back in my pockets.

"Where did you get this, anyway?"

I hesitated, unsure of how much to tell him, and knowing that anything I said would sound even more ridiculous now that he'd caught me trying to sneak something past him. Finally, I sighed and plopped myself down in the visitor's chair in front of the desk. "I got it from a guy who was walking by my van in the rain this morning."

"What guy?" As James sat forward, I could almost see him donning an invisible suit of armor.

"Just a guy. It was hailing, and . . ."

"You let a perfect stranger hang out with you in your truck to escape the weather?! What's wrong with you?"

"Nothing," I protested. "He didn't have a coat or an umbrella, and I'm a nice person."

James continued to glare at me, but I knew that deep down, he wanted to roll his eyes. His self-control in this area had me wondering if guys even know how to perform that particular ocular action.

"Why don't you just hand this over to your buddy, the detective?" he asked finally.

The tone of his question caught me by surprise. It was no secret that James and Luke weren't the best of friends, but I didn't understand why James sounded so testy. Much as I wanted to take a few minutes to give this some thought—or really anything that would keep me from talking—Idiot Ivy was in control. "I will if it turns out to be good information. I want to check it out first. If I simply hand it over to the cops, and it turns out to be nothing more than a wild goose chase, I could end up looking even guiltier than they think I am now. I've seen the truck the bad guys are using to drive around and pick up animals. I just want to see if it's parked out there or if there's any proof that's where they're taking them. I don't plan to get out of the vehicle."

Shaking his head, James refolded the map and tucked it in his shirt pocket. Before he could say anything else, the desk phone rang. He held up one finger in a request that I give him a moment then he focused his attention on his call.

While James spoke to his customer, I glanced around at the shelves behind him. There were pictures of his kids on the shelves behind him. There were pictures of the two girls – Janie and Jenny – together, and one of the two girls with their brother, Sam. Other photos in the array showed the kids in various activities, some individually, others as a group. James' kids ranged in ages from two to seven years older than

Anna. Since I never saw them, it was easy to forget that he had a family living in Houston. James and I had discussed his marriage a few times, and I was sure he'd made peace with his ex-wife and most of the associated demons. That said, I was still surprised to see more than one photo of the kids with their mother.

"There's no way I'm letting you go out there by yourself." These words were directed at me, startling me out of my musings. James paused, scowling at me and shaking his head. He heaved out an exasperated breath and said, "Do you have something to keep you busy and out of trouble for a few hours?"

I caught my bottom lip between my teeth to keep myself from talking, then I nodded.

"I'll meet you at your house between two-thirty and three, and we'll go from there."

"Really?" I squealed, failing miserably at hiding my happiness. As an afterthought, I added, "But why so late?"

"It won't do any good for us to get out there too early. Most people with regular jobs work until four or five. If the person doing this is casing houses, he'll want to be out of the neighborhoods before four to reduce the chances of someone seeing him." He paused and looked around the office. "I've got a kid from the high school who comes over to work in the afternoons after school. He's not in class this week, but he still won't be here until mid-afternoon. I can't leave until he gets here."

I really hated how logical he sounded. "You won't go without me, will you?"

James made a face, silently mimicking me. When he finally made noise, he said, "I'm not sure it's a good idea for either of us to go, but no, I won't go without you."

"Okay," I conceded. "Can I have my map back?"

"No!" He looked at me like he'd actually witnessed my brain sliding out of my ear.

"Fine. I'll see you at my house in a little while." I turned on my heel, fully intending to get away before he changed his mind. Unfortunately, my feet got tangled, sending me into the office's front door with a hollow-sounding *bonk*. Hoping to make it look like I hadn't just tripped over nothing, I leaned against the door and turned back toward the desk. "Before I forget, you wouldn't happen to know who plowed my garden for me, would you."

James shook his head at he as he stood. "Go home, Ivy. And try to not to hurt yourself."

On a typical day, I would have had at least two more appointments, but on this day, I had an open afternoon. I decided to go home, check on Ebony and the dogs, and maybe get some housekeeping chores done.

The wind was picking up again, bringing with it cooler temperatures and more storm clouds. I'd barely managed to get to the shelter of the porch before it started raining again. Ordinarily, Baskin would have been circling my feet to let me know everything on the premises was safe and secure, but this time he was nowhere to be seen. I stood on the stoop whistling for him, but the wind carried the sound away as soon as the air left my mouth. After a few useless calls, I went inside, where Robin pranced around near the door until

I gave her a welcoming rub. Seconds later, Ebony appeared. Based on the direction from which he'd swooped, I guessed he'd been at his dining room play area watching the trees blowing in the wind.

"Hello, honey," he said after landing on my shoulder.

Thunder rumbled outside, sending the easily frightened Robin to her favorite shelter under Anna's bed.

With Ebony on my shoulder, I went to the back porch to call Baskin again. His lack of response shouldn't have bothered me since it *was* pouring down rain. Unlike the skittish Robin, Baskin was not afraid of loud noises. He was not the biggest fan of water, but rain rarely kept him from responding to my calls. Still, something felt... off.

The combination of Ebony's sweetness, my increasing worries about my dog, and the storm outside made me not want to do housework—you know, more than usual. Instead, I sat down next to the window, got Ebony situated in my lap, and rubbed his neck while the storm swept closer. Dark, ominous clouds rolled in while windswept trees bowed deferentially before them. It wasn't long before lightning was flashing, drawing cries of "Weee!" from the bird in my lap.

Torrential rain prevented me from seeing farther than a few inches from the window. Once I got to thinking about it, I realized I knew very little about my outside dog's daily habits. He was familiar with my routines and likely knew that once the big purple box had left the yard, I wouldn't return for some time. Being canine, Baskin wouldn't understand the disruption in my schedule. I didn't know if he was the type of dog who turned into an explorer when left to his own devices. It was entirely possible that he had simply been caught away from the house and was waiting for the storm to pass before coming home. Baskin was microchipped and wore a collar with my name and number on one of his tags. No one had ever complained about him, but then there weren't that many people living in the area, and I doubted that the neighboring cows had access to phones. That thought generated a picture in my head of a cow trying to hold a cell phone in one front hoof, attempting to push buttons with the other. The result of this mental mini-movie was a very frustrated bovine.

I smiled to myself and sighed, vowing to find some type of tracker that would fit on Baskin's collar and map out his daily excursions. Holding Ebony up near my face, I said to him, "Surely, there's an app for that."

My bird's response was nothing more than a full-body shake followed by a fluffing out of his feathers.

With the stout winds, the weather was soon past us, taking with it my excuse to sit and brood. Reluctantly, I set Ebony back on his perch and gave him a treat. I forced myself to sweep, then to clean out the refrigerator before Wednesday's trash collection and wash the few dishes I'd neglected since Saturday morning. Even after my musings and the chores, I ended up with well over an hour before James' earliest estimated arrival time. Since I couldn't get my mind off Daryl's map, I decided to sit down at my computer and do a little remote sleuthing.

Google Maps is a wonderful thing for both a bored mind and one who easily gets lost. I can claim both of these afflictions, so that particular program is one of my best friends. I typed our county's name into the search line and waited while I was zipped past the virtual Earth and came to a gliding halt above a red dot in a sea of green. Using what I could remember of the map's details, I zoomed in, panned left, and refined my search until I could see the squiggly lines marked with the names and road numbers from the drawing.

Two things immediately presented themselves as problems. First, the trees in that area had grown together so densely that a satellite view didn't show much of anything except greenness. The second was that there was no County Road 515. We have a CR15, and a long, winding, branching CR51. CR15 is on the south end of the county, far away from where I was searching, so I focused on County Road 51. Again, though, the thicket in that area prevented aerial photos of anything other than the forest, and the street views seemed to be more computer-generated than live shots, so I guessed that whoever did the drive-around in our area hadn't ventured out to cover the smaller backroads. With a heavy sigh, I abandoned my remote search and went outside to feed my chickens.

When I stepped outside, I quickly noticed how much the temperature had changed. Since I hadn't had the forethought to don a coat, I welcomed the relative warmth of the coop. I made sure the biddies were content and well supplied for the night, then hurried back in the house. By the time James pulled into my driveway, you could feel the chill seeping in around the door. I grabbed a hooded jacket and jumped off the front porch before he came to a full stop. I earned a semi-disgusted look when I climbed in the pickup, though I don't know if it was because of my eagerness or the journey we were about to undertake.

"You do realize this will probably be a wasted trip, right?" he asked before setting his truck in motion again.

"Maybe."

"What's your plan if there isn't a white pickup parked out there?"

"I just want to see what everything looks like, you know, for my peace of mind. Even if there is no actual vehicle, there should be some sign of people coming and going. I want to take a couple of pictures on my phone, enough to make the police willing to investigate it further." Okay, to be honest, I hadn't known what I was going to say until the words started tumbling out of my mouth. I guess Non-Idiot Ivy was currently running the show. Then the words "Baskin is missing" burst from my lips.

James glanced over at me, a brief look of confusion- or was it concern?-dashing across his face. "What makes you think he's missing?"

"He wasn't here when I got home and didn't come when I called."

James nodded and continued backing out of the driveway. "I'm sure he's fine. He's probably curled up in a warm spot someplace waiting for the weather to clear."

Instead of responding, I studied the brush beside the road, searching for even the smallest hint of my dog's reddish-brown coat.

The county road we were looking for wasn't one of those that connects to the main highway. According to the map on my phone, we would have to follow a couple of minor roads before we arrived at any of the junctions with County Road 51. I wondered if James had looked up any maps since I'd seen him. I decided to wait until we were at least on the right side of town before I mentioned the possibility of an error in our directions.

"I can hear the wheels turning in your head, Ivy. What are you plotting?"

"Nothing."

I thought I sounded perfectly innocent and reasonable, but apparently, James' ears were sharper than mine. He turned to glare at me long enough that I began to worry about us staying on the road.

"The . . ." I stammered, pointing at the approaching curve.

He barely blinked and executed the turn without incident, stopping at the intersection to await my response.

"I promise. I'm not plotting anything." This, of course, was the truth. Withholding information was far from "plotting." In fact, it was almost the exact opposite. To emphasize my sincerity, I held up my right hand as though I was being sworn in at court.

"I can't wait until Anna starts trying to get around you," he mumbled as he checked the traffic.

I looked out the window and allowed myself the briefest of grins.

We traveled without conversation for several minutes. I'd like to say it was a comfortable silence, but there were too many thoughts running around in my head. At one point, I even considered the idea that the wheels James had referred to earlier were adding a charge to the tension in the air between us.

"Did you bring the map?" I asked, finally.

James scowled at me while he pulled the paper from his shirt pocket. It didn't appear that he'd looked at it after I'd left. He held it between his thumb and forefinger, just out of my reach.

"Why do you want it?"

I rolled my eyes. It's what girls do.

"Unlike you, I haven't had unlimited time to study it. I had *work* to do after it was given to me. I just want to see where we're going."

"I had work to do, too," he grumbled as he handed the page over to me.

I unfolded the paper and held it closer to my face than was probably necessary. The locations of the state highway and the first adjoining farm-to-market—also known as FM—road looked familiar. I gave James the names of the streets so he would know where to go, then I went back to studying the drawing. The place where Daryl had written in the county road number was smudged, as though the pen had coughed up extra ink or he'd come to the edge of the stable writing surface. I scratched at the mark but didn't see any change.

"I don't think this is County Road 515," I blurted, surprising myself.

"What?"

I looked over at James. "I don't think this third number is five. It's more like an S or something."

The laughter that tumbled from his mouth was even more of a shock than my own words. "I don't think there is such a thing as County Road 51S. There might be an A, a B, or a C after the number, but I seriously doubt there are enough places one road branches off that they'd ever get to the letter S."

I really wanted to stick my tongue out at him.

"Okay, well, I looked at a map while I was at home, and there is no County Road 515. There's a 51, and a 15, but County Road 15 is way down south. I think the guy who drew this was guessing at the road number."

"So, what makes you think he wasn't making all of this up?"

I shrugged. "I don't know, but we're almost to the turn-off, so we might as well keep going."

James flashed another undecipherable look at me but didn't comment further. A few minutes later, we turned on to a two-lane blacktop road that served as FM1316. It was bumpy, narrow, and the ditches on either side looked very wet. I tossed out a quick prayer, asking God to make the county road in question at least passable.

A few minutes later, my prayer was answered when we came to an intersection with CR51, a surprisingly wide oil-topped road.

"You have the map," James said, bringing his pickup to a stop. "Do we go right or left?"

I didn't have to look at the map to answer him. I gave him a cheesy smile and told him to turn right.

After the first twenty yards or so, the trees and brush became so thick that you'd never know civilization was only a few miles away. Unlike FM1316, which was bordered by pastureland and the occasional home place, County Road 51 looked almost like virgin timber land. If not for the barbed-wire fencing strung between both posts and tree trunks, the road itself would have been the only clue that man had ever set foot here. The daylight began to wane as we drove, which only complicated matters further.

"Looks like we've got more rain coming in," James

commented as I glanced up through the windshield. I must have looked worried, because he added, "You do know this is a four-wheel-drive, right? You don't have to worry about getting stuck."

I breathed a sigh of relief.

Several minutes later, we passed an abrupt clearing. James slowed down so I could get a good look, but he didn't stop completely. I spotted a structure set back from the road several yards, with a sign in front declaring it as the future home of a Sack-n-Track convenience store. This was not the old, covered arena I'd expected after my conversation with Daryl. It was a much smaller building with a battered shingle roof. There was a large window covered on the inside with black material, and a big piece of corrugated metal tacked up over what was likely a doorframe. A handful of scrub trees crowded one end of the hut, while the other had construction screening tacked to old posts to form a type of privacy fence. The ground in the clearing was marked with potholes and ruts, but the day's rain had made it impossible to tell if any of the wear was new.

"No, wait!" I exclaimed as the truck began to pick up speed again.

"I'm just going to see what else is down here," James answered. "We'll come back."

I nodded but turned to look over my shoulder at the building as it disappeared behind a wall of timber. As we drove, we encountered a private road on the left that was blocked by a gate, and an unmarked, two-lane dirt track on the right. After several more minutes of thick trees and underbrush, the only thing we found was a dilapidated old house in the midst of being reclaimed by the forest.

"I find it hard to believe that someone wants to put a convenience store out here," James commented as he executed a three-point turn.

"Well, the sign didn't look all that new," I offered.

"Yeah, but that mesh stuff around the side of the building was in too good a shape to have been there very long. I want to see what else is down that other road."

James shifted his pickup into four-wheel-drive before we turned down the muddy track of the unmarked road. We passed the entrance to another tract of land on the right, one that had been clear-cut in the recent past and had a gate set back from the road. After driving a little farther, it became apparent that there wasn't much else to be found. Without another word, we turned around again and pulled as close to the open land as the gate would allow.

From our new vantage point, we could just see a small portion of the building in question. There appeared to be a window, though from where we sat, I couldn't tell if it was covered with something or just really dirty. James fished around under his seat until he came up with a pair of binoculars. A light rain began to fall as he focused on the structure.

"Can you see if that's a window?" I asked, straining to look through the growing darkness. As if the foliage and the fading light weren't making things difficult enough, condensation began to form on the windows.

"I can't really see anything, Ivy," he answered grumpily. "Maybe if you'd stop breathing, the windows wouldn't fog up."

I glared at him, earning a laugh before he reached

for the vehicle's defroster.

"We're not going to find much proof of anything today. We can't park anywhere with a view of the front without being seen, and the rain has washed away any tracks that might have been made before today." James set the binoculars down and shook his head. Looking chagrined, he said, "I'm afraid you're just going to have to give the map to Swaim and let him deal with it."

I knew he was right, but I didn't want to accept it. "Do you really think he'll investigate this place based on my word, a kind of crappy map, and some construction fence?"

James shrugged. "I don't know. Way out here, he'll probably do what we did and drive by. It's more likely he'll hand it off to the sheriff's office and let them check it out."

"But . . ." I started to protest but had no words.

"I'm sorry, Ivy."

Disappointed, I nodded, while James put the pickup in gear to back away from the fence. As we began to reverse, I noticed a tree that had fallen across the barbed wire nearby. It occurred to me that the narrow trail that afforded us the limited view of the back of the hut was wide enough to get me through the thick undergrowth. There was also plenty of cover to hide in if someone happened to look out or see me. Without giving myself time to chicken out, I released my seatbelt and jumped from the truck.

"Ivy!"

I heard James call my name as the door closed behind me, and I knew by the sound of the tires on the mud that he'd slammed on the brake. I tip-toed through a puddle and started climbing the tree trunk. The bark was slippery from the rain, but I managed to hang on long enough to clear the fence and jump down on the other side. The trail I'd thought would be wide enough for me to navigate seemed to close up on me, and my coat kept snagging on twigs and thorns. Too soon, the path ended at a muddy clearing, several feet from the back of the building. I hesitated. The only sounds I could hear were the raindrops falling on the sparse leaves and my own breathing. Off to the right, I could still make out the material they'd used as a fence. Even though I knew there was a clearing and a road beyond it, nothing was visible other than the dark netting.

I heard a crash behind me, followed by a whispered curse. I knew James was coming to collect me, and I couldn't let him take me away before I'd had a chance to get closer and maybe peek in the window. I glanced left, then took off for the building's back wall. The mud squished under my feet, making me slip several times. When I approached the wall, I tried to stop, but ended up sliding until I hit the wood siding with a muffled *Thump!*

I froze, listening for sounds of footsteps or shouts from inside the building. What I heard was a series of muffled barks, followed by one long, low howl. I was sure it was Bentley baying, and he didn't sound happy. Fueled by the lonely sound, I became even more determined to have a look through the window. A hand spun me around as I started moving to my left.

"Ivy! Are you crazy? What do you think you're doing?"

James was close enough to me that his breath warmed my face.

"Listen," I whispered back. We waited a moment

but only heard silence.

"You have gone out of your ever-lovin' mind. We need to get out of here."

"No! I heard dogs in there. I want to look in the window."

"And how are you going to do that?"

When James gestured, I looked around to see that the window was at least a foot over my head.

"You can give me a boost," I suggested.

"No, what I need to do is throw you over my shoulder and haul your—" More barks issued from inside the building, interrupting whatever he was going to say. He stilled for a moment, then motioned for me to move. "Fine. I'll lift you up enough for a quick look, but then we really have to get out of here."

I nodded and approached the window. Even staying close to the building, the mud caused my feet to shift without warning. James swore under his breath as he tried to find his own solid footing. Finally, I felt his hands on my waist as he began to lift me up to the filthy window. I got one partial peek into the room before a couple of things happened. First, the sound of a car door slamming reached our ears, seeming to come from the front of the structure. Then, at about the same time, James must have slipped because I suddenly dropped to the ground, banging my head against the wall. The barking that erupted from inside could have been the result of either noise—or both—but we weren't hanging around to find out. Before I could finish my next breath, James had me by the hand and was tugging me toward the trees.

We all grow up on stories of super-human strength that infuses ordinary mortals in times of peril. I don't know if James' strength was affected, but he definitely wasn't having any trouble navigating the muck between the hut and brush. I, of course, wasn't as fortunate. Halfway across the expanse, the mud gripped my right shoe and wouldn't let go. Completely unaware of my predicament, James plowed forward. I'm sure if someone had been watching, I would have made a comical sight: one foot mired in brown goo, one hand in the iron grip of a charging bear of a man and dangling in between was little old me.

My shoe eventually gave up its hold on my appendage. The sudden release seemed to sling-shot me into the back of James' leg, which made him stumble, though he didn't go down. Instead, he continued to motor forward, dragging me along until he'd found enough cover to conceal us from sight.

"What the—?" Once on semi-solid ground, James turned to me and very nearly rolled his eyes. He helped me to my feet, muttering about hard-headed women and mud.

"Shhh!" I urged.

The racket in the building behind us drowned out whatever noise he was making.

"Did you see Baskin?" he asked as he led the way back to the downed tree.

"No. I didn't have time to see much of anything. There were so *many* dogs!"

Shaking his head at me, James said, "I tried to tell you this would be a waste of time."

"It wasn't a waste," I protested. "I heard Bentley. I saw dogs. We found them!"

"I ought to make you ride in the bed of the truck," he grumbled as he helped me over the fence.

Chapter 16

Back at my house we had a brief argument about what to do next. I ended up sending Detective Swaim a text, telling him I had information about his investigation and asking him to meet me at my house at 7:00 p.m. James and I parted ways in my driveway.

If I stayed too long under the hot stream of water in my shower, it wasn't because I didn't have a good reason. I was cold enough that I was sure my bone marrow was on the verge of turning into icicles, and while the heat wasn't enough to completely warm my insides, I knew it would eventually seep past my stubborn soft tissues. Besides, half the mud in my hair was comprised of clay, so the only way to get it out was to loosen it with water.

Once out of the shower, I dressed in layers—athletic tights under my sweatpants, turtleneck under a long-sleeved shirt, and two pairs of socks. I don't like being cold, and I wanted to make sure that none of my shower warmth escaped into the atmosphere. I put my muddy clothes in the washer to soak in spite of the fact that I was sure I'd never get the reddish mud stains out of anything I'd been wearing.

Ebony stayed on my shoulder while I moved about the house, and Robin stayed on my heels. Instead of making myself a decent supper, I made hot chocolate from scratch. I brooded over the events of the afternoon while I stirred my cocoa.

The scene I'd viewed from my brief peek in the window was a lot to take in. In a nutshell, it had been a horrible sight. The dogs were being kept in a small room, one about half the size of the office at James' garage. There had been at least a dozen dogs in there, all drinking from one bucket of water and prancing through everyone else's waste. The only door had been little more than a frame with chicken wire attached to keep the dogs in. I hadn't had time to assess the health of any of the animals, but I knew there were a few smaller dogs that would have had trouble getting to the water even if the bucket had been full. I could only guess at how they were being fed—if they were being fed at all.

I pulled Robin up in the chair with me when I settled in the living room to wait for Swaim. It broke my heart to think of those dogs being forced to leave their comfy, loving homes only to be dumped in a dirty, smelly room with only the barest necessities. Every fiber in my body screamed at me to go help those dogs—now, not later—and to let the police catch up whenever they could. Common sense and a sweet, wiggly dog kept me rooted in place.

A few minutes before seven, James came to the door. Baskin was still absent, and my concern for him was growing by the second. Before I could do more than wave him toward a chair, an assertive rap on my door caused us both to jump. I answered the knock without looking outside and found The Swami on my porch. When he stepped into the living room, he seemed surprised to see James in my living room. The two men greeted each other with a civilized handshake, but their mutual distrust of each other gave the air an extra zip of electricity. James sat in a chair near the window, while Luke perched on the end of the couch nearest the door. Since I was already agitated, I remained standing. Still, with the tension between the two, my hair was almost standing on end. Even Ebony found the room uncomfortable. Out of the blue, my bird declared, "Bedtime, honey!" hopped to the floor, and disappeared down the hallway.

"Okay, Ivy, I'm here. What kind of information do you have for me?" Detective Swaim's posture displayed relaxed confidence that would have been appropriate for a casual visit. His expression, however, showed barely concealed impatience with a hint of suspicion.

All of my inner Ivys banded together to blurt, "I think Baskin was stolen."

Swaim raised a cynical eyebrow at me. "What makes you think that?"

"A dog didn't bark at you when you got out of your car, did it?" James delivered this question with enough of an attitude that even a block of cement would have picked up on his tone.

Luke scowled but otherwise ignored James' comment.

"Baskin always hangs around the house, especially when I'm home." I saw no reason to mention my earlier ponderings about the possibility that my dog might patrol the adjoining properties while I was in town. "I saw him this morning before I left and haven't seen him since. I've been home most of the day, and he hasn't come any of the times I've called."

Swaim considered this information, nodded, then shrugged. "Okay, I'll add him to the list of missing animals. Why don't you text me his description and anything else you think might be of importance?"

His words and overall posture practically screamed that he felt like I'd wasted his time. When he moved to stand, I put my hand up in front of him in a gesture that was identical to the one I used when telling a dog to stay.

"Wait." My mouth suddenly went dry. "I know where the pets— at least the dogs—that were taken are being held."

"Oh?" That one word contained enough sarcasm to coat the inside of a football stadium. "Before I ask how you know this, I need to be sure that you don't want your lawyer present. I don't want there to be any confusion later."

I hesitated. I hadn't even thought to ask Daddy to come out for this.

"I hardly think that's necessary," James interjected. "Ivy is coming forward as a private citizen to help you with a case. Besides, she may also be a victim."

The look Luke tossed at James stopped just short of a sneer. "Well, you're here. Maybe you'd like a lawyer, too. I believe it's the same man, right?"

"You two need to stop," I said, hoping to head off an argument before it started. In the back of my mind, I wondered if it wouldn't have been easier to speak to Swaim alone. "James is here because he was with me when I found the dogs. I know where they are, and I know they're scared and dirty and probably cold, and they all need to go home as soon as possible. Luke, I need your help. *They* need your help."

My personalized plea seemed to have the desired effect. The detective eased back on the couch, nodded, gestured with his hand, and said, "Okay, Ms. Ivy. Tell me what you've got."

I started by reminding him of the truck I'd seen and how it compared with those used by PAWS. Then I mentioned my conversation with Daryl (without offering his name and our location at the time), the map he'd given me, and how I'd come to peek inside the hut in the woods. As I spoke, Swaim began to inch forward on the seat cushion. By the time I got to the part about peeking through the window, he appeared ready to leap to his feet. I left out the bit about losing my shoe and knee-skiing through the mud.

"What were you thinking?" Swaim was talking to James. "I understand that she doesn't always have access to common sense—"

"Hey!" I protested.

"—but I would have thought you would know better than to go running around on someone else's property, looking in their windows."

Seemingly unaffected by the detective's implication, James shrugged. "I knew she'd go out there by herself and probably find more trouble than she could handle. I went along to make sure she got home in one piece."

Swaim dropped his head, shaking it slowly in defeat.

In hopes of helping, I added, "If it hadn't been for

James lifting me, I wouldn't have been able to see in the window. We wouldn't have proof."

"What proof?" Luke asked, skewering me with cold, blue eyes. "Did you take a picture? Grab some hair samples? Or did you only leave fingerprints?"

Okay, now I felt a little stupid.

"Did you *see* your dog?"

Dejected, I shook my head and looked down at my feet.

"I have a picture," James said. "I got a shot of the vehicle parked in front of the building before we left. It's the same white pickup Ivy described earlier."

"Send me that photo," Swaim said. He took a business card from his pocket as he got to his feet. He paced a few steps before turning back to me. "What happened to the map?"

"It's in my coat pocket," I answered. I pivoted on my heel, ready to sprint to the laundry room. With slightly less enthusiasm, I stopped and turned to face my guests. "Well, it *was* in my coat pocket, which means it's now in the wash with the rest of my clothes."

James smothered a chuckle as Luke's phone chimed with the receipt of the new message. With his eyes still glittering with merriment, James said, "I can lead you back out to the building, then you can take it from there."

Distracted by the photo he'd just received, Swaim nodded.

I found his response encouraging, so I said, "Great! I'll go get my coat."

In unison, both men said, "You're not going."

"But . . ." My protest ran out of gas even before it cleared my lips.

One look between my two guests was enough for them to negotiate a truce and come up with a plan for who was in charge and how they would leave me out of the rest of the investigation.

"You aren't going anywhere near that place," Swaim said, pointing his finger at me. "Williamson and I will go out there first thing in the morning and see what we can see."

"No!" I protested again. "You can't wait until tomorrow."

He ignored me. Turning to James, he said, "It's probably too wet to go out there now. Let's meet up at eight in the morning. Maybe the wind will dry things out enough by then that my cruiser won't get stuck."

James shook his head. "The road is in good shape; your car won't have any trouble. The thing is, we don't know how much longer they'll keep those dogs there. Some have been gone almost a week, maybe more. They could move them or do whatever they're going to do at any time."

My eyes bounced between the two men. James was now on the edge of his chair, ready to move when given the signal. Swaim seemed to be weighing his options. I decided to tip the scales in favor of going sooner rather than later.

"If you wait until tomorrow, I'm going out there myself. I'll go tonight and get every one of those dogs out of there before anything else happens to them."

Luke nailed me with another icy glare. After a lengthy internal debate, he pointed a finger at me but turned to look at James. "Are you sure you can find this place in the dark?"

"Of course. I grew up here. I know these backroads

well enough I could find it blindfolded."

I nearly started to point out that he hadn't known precisely which county road we'd been looking for or what lay at the end of each of the lanes when we'd been out there earlier, but I managed to keep my mouth shut. I wanted Luke to investigate our claims more than I wanted to wipe the smugness off of my neighbor's face.

"Okay. We'll go now, in my car. After that, I'll decide how to proceed, and you'll both stay out of it. Ivy, go get your coat."

I muttered a *yippee!* as I hopped up from the couch.

Swaim added, "You're only going because I don't trust you to stay here until we get back."

Following a suggestion from James, I had to sit in the back seat—where the doors have safety locks and can only be opened from the outside. I was less than happy about this, but I was allowed to go along, so I could hardly complain. Thirty minutes and two wrong turns later, we cruised past the shack with its hopeful-yet-false signage. The building appeared to be entirely dark, and the fake Pinnacle Animal Control truck was parked at an angle, nose-in to the fencing, where the lettering on the doors would be hard to see from the road. After a brief discussion in the front seat about the beat-up little car James had seen with the pickup earlier, we turned around and went back to my house. Having done his part, James went home. After depositing me in my living room again, the detective made me swear I would stay home and not meddle in the rest of his investigation. Before leaving, he promised me the dogs would not be forced to remain in their prison for more than another twelve to fifteen hours.

Chapter 17

"Hi, Mama, how was your day?"

Anna's voice sounded almost like it would on any typical day, yet there was just a hint of something else, something held back. I was curious, but I didn't want to rush her.

"My day was okay, I guess. Nothing special." Since I'd sat in my van with a stranger who liked to run around and flash his business at little old ladies, I knew this statement was more than just a little white lie. I didn't even consider mentioning our missing mutt. I sent a prayer to God, asking for forgiveness, then asked my daughter about her day.

"Oh, you know . . ." She was trying so hard to be casual, but her excitement quickly bubbled over. "We found NEMO!"

"Nemo?" We've seen Nemo's movie at least a hundred times, but I knew if I played dumb, it would add a little spice to my daughter's story. "Is that some little boy who got lost?"

My feigned idiocy was rewarded with a delighted laugh.

"No, Mama, the fish! You know, Nemo, from the movie!"

"Oh! *That* Nemo. I didn't know he'd gone missing again."

Anna giggled some more. "I think he gets lost every day, but people always find him."

Her answer made me chuckle. "And today it was you who got to find him? Where were you?"

"Well, it was me, and Grandmom, and Granddaddy, and about ten other people who were there. We went to a place called Ep-Cot today." She pronounced the name of Epcot carefully, as though she was tasting a new flavor of ice cream. "There was so much to do there! Nemo and Dory have their own building, and you go in and get to ride around in the middle of the coral. And . . ."

I listened with half an ear while she told me all about the world created around Nemo by the people of Disney. I was happy that she was having such a great time and more than a little comforted that she was far away from Baskin's disappearance and the pet-napping that was happening in our town. Another thought flickered at the edge of my consciousness, slipping away with my daughter's next comment.

"That's when we found Nemo. His dad worries about him a lot." Anna's report ended on a note of censure, most likely because she has been scolded before for causing me concern.

"I'm sure he does if his baby fish gets lost every single day. I know I would worry if you got lost."

"But I wouldn't be in the ocean."

I love the simple logic of a kid.

"So, is that all you did today?"

"No, we were a lot busier than that. We got to go to all these different little cities that were like other countries."

Ebony fluttered in from the dining room, landing on my lap gracefully. He eyed the phone in my hand, cocked his head as if to listen, then settled himself down for a neck rub. We practiced this ritual almost nightly. Granted, I usually wasn't on the phone, but this was his way of exchanging pleasantries before he went to bed.

". . . and I saw Donald Duck wearing a big Mexican hat!"

"A sombrero?"

"Yes! He looked so funny!"

She continued to recount her afternoon adventures while I tried to focus on what she was saying. The sound of her voice was like a salve to my abraded emotions. I looked down at the bird in my lap and wondered what I would do if anyone ever took him away from me. Ebony had been part of my life almost as long as Anna. He was smart and funny, possessing more personality than one might expect from a bird. Had my bird been human, Ebony would forever be about three years old—old enough to grasp many of the emotions people express, yet not quite developed enough to understand the reasons behind them. He would not understand if he were suddenly taken away from us, and I had no doubt he would suffer some trauma if he were forced to stay in a cage all the time. Some birds turn to self-mutilation when faced with abrupt life changes, like moving to a new home with unfamiliar people. It broke my heart to think of this beautiful bird plucking out his snowy-white feathers.

I tuned back into Anna when her voice stopped.

"That sounds so exciting! What was your favorite part?"

"The best, very, very best part was this ride we went on. Aunt Gina and Uncle Jace took me on it, and it was like we were flying! We went all over the world and saw things like polar bears and elephants!"

"You've gotten to see a lot of elephants on this trip, haven't you?"

"Uh-huh, but these weren't real. It was like being inside a movie but flying." Anna paused to take a breath. "Oh, and we saw all these really pretty boats. They were all sorts of colors. Well, the boats weren't, really, but they used these big sheets to catch the wind, and those were all colorful."

"It sounds like you had a full day."

"Oh, Mama, when we started flying, my head started spinning like it does when I get off the merry-go-round at the park. It was so cool!"

I wasn't sure I liked the idea of a flying ride that made her head spin, and I suddenly pictured Anna stumbling around with pictures whizzing past her. "You got dizzy? Are you okay?"

"Oh, yes! It went away real quick, and it was just at the very beginning, but it made it so much fun!"

"Oh, okay," I answered, breathing a sigh of relief. "Did Cody go on this ride, too?"

"No, he didn't want to. Grandmom and Granddaddy stayed with him because they didn't want to go on that kind of a ride, either." The pleasure and excitement in her voice were supplemented with pride. "I think he was scared of going flying, but I wasn't. I'm really glad, too, because it was *so cool*!"

I had to chuckle at her enthusiasm.

"I'm so glad you had a good day," I said with genuine feeling.

"Me, too," Anna said with a happy breath. After a brief pause, she asked, "So, what did you really do today, Mama?"

"Well . . ." Mentally, I answered, *I went with James to a shack in the woods, I trespassed on someone else's land, thought about breaking into a horrible little building, and lost my shoe in a giant mud puddle . . .* Out loud, I said, "It rained today and stormed a little this morning, but we're all okay. I worked."

"Did you see Bentley? And take him for a training walk?"

"I did see Bentley today, but we didn't go for a walk." At least this was mostly true.

"Oh, because of the rain, right?"

"Uh-huh," I answered vaguely.

"Did you see Mr. James today? Or Detective Luke?"

"I saw both. They each asked me to tell you 'hi' for them."

"Okay!" Anna sounded genuinely pleased. "I didn't have a lot of time today, but when I woke up, I thought about God promising stuff and how Miss Fuentes used to tell us that if something God tells us doesn't come true, it's probably because we made the wrong choice."

"Oh." I had trouble forming a response because I wasn't sure how I felt about this particular message. Miss Fuentes had been Anna's Arts and Religion teacher the previous fall. She was a good teacher, but very young, and she still had quite a bit to learn. While I wanted Anna to give thought to her choices when making them, I wasn't sure I wanted her to think that God would withhold something from her because she decided on one option over another. "Well, I have another Bible verse if you want to try it out."

"Oh, yes, please!"

"Okay, this one is from Matthew. It says, 'Judge not, that ye not be judged.'"

"Hmm," she said thoughtfully. "Is it a judge like what Grandfather and Aunt Win like to argue with when they go to court?"

I swallowed a chuckle. "No, not that kind of judge. When they go to court, the judge is a person doing a job. In this Bible verse, 'judge' is an action word. It means to look at what someone else is doing and decide you can do it better than they can, even before you try it."

We repeated the verse together before Anna said, "They mean that we shouldn't be snooty because we wouldn't like it if someone was snooty to us?"

There was no stifling my amusement this time. "Yes, baby. Exactly."

"Hmm . . . okay. I'll think about that one, too."

"Thinking about it is a good idea."

"Mama, is it okay if I say my prayers now? I'm kinda tired, and tomorrow is our last day here, so I want to feel good."

"That's perfectly fine, Anna Claire. Pray away."

In an increasingly sleepy voice, my daughter thanked God for James, Detective Luke, the ride at Epcot that made her feel like she was flying, and for all the people in her family. Then she asked Him to watch over all the animals (everywhere) and to please stop Nemo from getting lost tomorrow so his dad wouldn't worry.

It wasn't until after we'd hung up for the night that I realized what idea had been teasing the edges of my brain. Anna traditionally calls both sets of grandparents "Grandmother" and "Grandfather" when addressing them in person. Over the last few days, she'd begun to call Mr. Greene "Granddaddy," and even more recently referred to Mrs. Greene as "Grandmom." I found it interesting that several days together had inspired my daughter to get less formal with Rex's parents. I didn't know if this was something they had requested or a natural response to spending so much time with them.

I was far too tired to give it much thought, so I pushed it from my mind.

Chapter 18

The whole purpose of sleep is to give the body and mind a chance to relax and recharge. The brain keeps working, of course, but active thoughts about world events are supposed to shift to the back burner. That isn't what I experienced Tuesday night.

After my call with Anna, I felt happy, calm, secure. The stress of the day, not to mention the rolling around in the mud, had made my body—and mind—tired and in need of rest. I should have been able to climb into bed and go right to sleep, but my brain had other ideas. As a result, the majority of my night was spent flip-flopping restlessly under the covers, trying to rid my thoughts of the slideshow of horrible things that may have—and could still—happen to those poor dogs. I had visions of skin-and-bones canines shivering in the cold and open wounds oozing into the night. Trust me when I say that those were the best of the images that haunted my mind's eye. Those few times I did get to sleep, my dreams were full of the same types of disturbing images. I didn't get any restful sleep until the time I would have been getting out of bed on a normal day. It was almost 7:30 a.m. when I finally crawled out from under the covers, feeling like I'd been beaten with a sack full of rocks.

Ebony perched on my shoulder for a ride through the house to get his breakfast. Being a bird, he didn't offer any comments about how I was dressed as I stumbled to the kitchen—fuzzy brown bear-claw slippers, a green long-sleeved night shirt with skiing polar bears, and a plush, rainbow-colored bathrobe with a unicorn hood. I have no doubt that my attire, combined with my Medusa hair, made me a sight to behold. I set water on to boil for my tea and wandered into the dining room to feed Ebony and Robin. In the span of about seventeen seconds, I got two surprises: the first came from the calendar when I saw the shamrock sticker that announced it was St. Patrick's Day. If Daryl's word was as good as his information, today would be his swansong before leaving Pinnacle. The second surprise came when Ebony flew into the living room to perch on the back of the couch and peck on the window. This isn't something he usually does, so I should have expected to see something unusual outside. However, my sluggish brain was slow to react, and I got a start when I saw a Pinnacle police car parked across the end of my driveway. This was odd, not least because I live outside the city limits, so technically it should have been a sheriff's car. Intent on discovering the reason for my roadside visitor, I forgot I wasn't exactly wearing pants when I opened the door. The cold air that rushed in reminded me.

Once I was more appropriately dressed and had wrangled my hair into a loose bun, I set out to discover the identity of the person in the cruiser. As I approached, the driver's window began to descend, and I recognized my friend, Officer Dennis March. He waved and offered me one of his trademark big smiles.

"Good morning, Ivy!" His enthusiasm poured from the car like soap bubbles from an over-filled tub.

"Hey, Dennis. What are you doing here?"

"The Swami sent me over to make sure you didn't get in the way of his stakeout this morning."

"Oh, really?" I crossed my arms over my ribs and arched an eyebrow at him. Dennis was looking into the sun, so he probably didn't see my scowl. "Why did he send you?"

"I volunteered," he answered proudly. "Detective Swami said he needed someone to come out and make sure you stayed home, but there weren't any takers. I think they're all afraid that your dad might come out here and get onto them. You and I never had any trouble, so I said I'd do it."

A pickup approached from my right. A quick tap of the horn drew my attention to James, who waved as he drove by. Given the hour, I guessed that he'd had a tough night, too, since James was usually headed into town by seven. Part of me wished he hadn't witnessed this particular spectacle, but most of me was thankful it was James and not some gossip from further down the road.

"How long have you been out here?" Considering the time, it seemed like a reasonable question.

"I got here about six," he answered, still smiling. "I don't think they were going to get set up on that old building until around seven, but he seemed to think you might be out and about early today."

I shook my head in disgust, internally denying that I would likely have done precisely that if I'd had a decent night's sleep. "What am I supposed to do if I have an eight o'clock client?"

"It would probably be best if you could reschedule it, but if not, I'm supposed to go with you and make sure you don't get into anything."

"Great," I said flatly. "Well, lucky for both of us, my morning is free. Why don't you come in? I'm just about to make breakfast. Can I make you some, too?"

"No, but thanks anyway, Ivy." Inside the car, Dennis held up a Styrofoam cup. "I grabbed breakfast on the way out here. I've still got plenty of coffee and everything. I should be set until the detective gives us the all-clear."

I nodded. It was a chilly morning, and while I had on warm clothes, I was ready to get back inside. "Well, let me know if you need anything, Dennis."

"Thank you, Ivy. I'll give you a shout when it's okay to carry on with your day."

I nodded and waved before turning to go back to the house.

I'm not accustomed to hanging around my house on any day except Saturday, and the fact that I was being told not to leave just made me feel more like a caged animal than a rational woman. I fed myself and my pets, frequently checking to see if Dennis was still in the driveway. I put the clothes that had been soaking on to wash, and generally just piddled around trying to keep myself busy. Ebony, sitting at his play area in the dining room, tracked my movements with great interest. Finally, just before nine, my phone rang.

"Good morning, Ms. Ivy." It was Detective Swaim.

"Was it really necessary to send someone out to block my driveway?" I could have returned his greeting a little more cordially, but all things considered, I was at least civil.

"Better to be safe than sorry," he answered. "Listen, I don't know what your schedule looks like today—"

"It's pretty bare, thanks to you," I interrupted. I honestly hadn't realized how annoyed I was until he called.

"Well, if you could clear whatever you have today, maybe put it off for another day, we could really use your help."

Those were the words I'm pretty sure he said; however, what I heard was more like, "Blah, blah, blah . . . your help."

"My help?" I repeated.

"Yes, ma'am. We've got quite an assortment of pets out here. Since you know just about everyone in town, I thought maybe you could help us identify their owners, and possibly even help us get some of them cleaned up before they go home."

A shot of pure adrenaline hit my system, a result of the sheer joy I experienced at hearing the dogs had been rescued. I tried to keep my voice level. "Yeah, sure. I can do that."

"Good deal. We've got several trucks headed over to the PAWS facility. They're going to evaluate the animals and see if any of them are microchipped. If you'll head that direction, I'll let them know to expect you."

"Okay." It felt like I was forgetting something, but whatever it was kept evading my mental spotlight. Then it hit me. "Does this mean you caught the guys?"

"Well, I can't get into specifics, but I can tell you that we have two men in custody. When they pulled in here this morning, they looked like they were getting ready to move the animals. It appears that we timed this just right."

"Okay then," I managed to squeak out when I realized he couldn't see me nodding over the phone. Since I was about to break into a happy dance, I was thrilled we didn't have a video connection.

Dennis offered to give me an escort to the PAWS facility complete with flashing lights, but I declined. Being seen following him (or him following me) would be enough to get many tongues wagging—again.

The scene at the shelter was organized chaos. My first objective was to locate Baskin. Each of the rescued animals was housed in some form of a travel cage. Some of these were wire, while others were of the hard plastic variety. We had to sort the containers by animal type, anyway, so I gave my fellow workers my dog's description and began working. By the time the animals were appropriately grouped, I'd counted about two dozen dogs, nearly ten cats, more than a dozen small rodents, four bunnies, two enormous snakes, and a single, very baffled piglet. Only about half of the pets had microchips, and of those remaining, I was able to help identify most of them. While volunteers called the contact numbers provided with the microchips, the rest assured each pet had water and then prioritized them by medical need. All were hungry, dirty, and slightly dehydrated, but otherwise in reasonably good health. It was only after all of this activity that I finally found my dog. Baskin was crouching in a hard-sided crate, his hind legs braced against the back wall, ready to spring for freedom as soon as someone unlatched the door.

Relief flowed from my eyes in the form of tears as I wrote my information on the card provided by the PAWS staff. Several people patted me on the back to express their joy for the recovery of my dog. With the claim form for Baskin completed, I spent a few minutes talking to him before going back to work.

A system was set up to route each pet to the appropriate person for evaluation. Those animals with apparent wounds would be seen by a veterinarian first. Any that were lacking noticeable issues would be checked by one of three available veterinary technicians. Each pet also had to be photographed for evidence once the case went to trial, so a Pinnacle PD officer was assigned to each veterinarian and technician. Once cleared by the vet tech, the docile ones and those who appeared the least traumatized were then funneled in my direction based on the premise that they would be less likely to bite. The regular PAWS staff had the pleasure of bathing the biters. Happily, Baskin was the first dog to come to me. I held him until he relaxed some, then put him in one of the dog crates I carry in my van. Baskin was able to see, hear, and smell me as I began work on the procession of his fellow captives. I recognized almost all of the dogs sent my direction, so the only thing that made this different from any other day was the volume (and the lack of pay, of course).

It wasn't until late morning that someone noticed the bunnies and other small rodents were highly agitated and that the piglet was squealing almost non-stop. We gathered around to brainstorm, but before the first idea was voiced, the facility vet pointed out that

the snakes—one banana python and one ball python—
were housed amid that collection of animals. The cute,
fuzzy pets were then dispersed among the people
operating the phones, which left the piglet, two rats, and
the snakes. I don't mind snakes, but I like them a lot
more when I don't have to look at or touch them, and
my only experiences with rats have been when they've
become a nuisance around the chickens or in my house,
and I always ask Baskin to help me with them. I
grabbed up the crate with the piglet and went back to
work, explaining to the person who asked that I have a
bird, so I'm accustomed to odd noises. Happily, the
piglet settled in nicely once it was placed in my van.

Bentley was among those without an identifier. He
was basking in the warmth of my canine blow dryer
when his people arrived. Becky was beside herself with
emotion, sobbing uncontrollably and hanging onto her
husband's arm for support. I would have shamed them
for not having Bentley chipped, but she was so wound
up that I didn't have the heart to do more than mention
it and promise to remind them again later. As if to make
up for all the commotion, Bentley acted like the model
dog when he left the PAWS facility. He walked quietly
next to Becky at the heel position, sat down and waited
when they reached the door, and didn't drag anyone to
the car once they were in the parking lot. The same
could not be said for the majority of the dogs leaving
the building.

On one of my many trips to and from my van to the
PAWS building, I ran into Detective Swaim. He asked
for a quick word with me before pulling me to the side
and out of the way of the foot traffic. The dog I had just
finished grooming was only about twelve pounds, so I

held the happy little pup instead of making it stand around and wait for us to finish our chat. Based on the satisfied grunts coming from the dog's mouth, I didn't think she minded the extra attention.

"How are things going?" Luke asked, suddenly seeming more like his usual charming self and less like a hassled police detective. He reached out to pet the pooch.

I was wet—both from sweat and dogs shaking water on me—smelled funny, and my feet were tired. In other words, I was in hog heaven. I grinned, but still kept up my guard. It had been a long couple of days.

"Great," I answered. "I'm so glad you got out there when you did. It's heartbreaking to think about what might have happened to all these babies if you hadn't rescued them."

He paused, looking uncharacteristically uneasy, then continued. "Well, I *did* have some help," he said, "and a lot of that help came from you, Ms. Ivy."

To my embarrassment, I felt my face flush. Was I so easily won over? I recalled sitting in the interrogation room with Luke and my dad, feeling exposed and vulnerable under Luke's careless cross-examination. I squirmed a little and focused my attention on the pooch in my arms.

"Did you find your dog?"

"I did!" My response was only a sliver of an octave lower than a squeal. "He was dirty and hungry, but otherwise he seems to be fine."

"That's great. I'm glad to hear it." Luke's words and expression sounded genuine, but at the same time, he seemed to be holding something back. Finally, he asked, "Are you still upset with me?"

When I didn't answer immediately, he added, "Over my questioning last weekend?"

"Well, if you want to know the truth, yes. I still can't believe that you felt you had to ask for the details of my husband's death. Not only were your questions completely irrelevant to your investigation, your accusations were hurtful." If Luke was surprised by the intensity of my anger, he wasn't alone. I hadn't realized that I was still holding onto so many negative feelings. I wanted to stop talking and end the discomfort for both of us, but there was still so much to say. "And then you had to bring up my finances and the Gentry Trust. You swoop in and dig around in my business and air out the details until I look like some shady criminal. I've worked really hard to make something of myself in this town. I do good work, and I'm a good person. My past and my finances are *my* business, mine to announce or keep to myself. You had no right! Now I'll have to explain it all to my dad. So yes, I was upset—I'm still upset." Running out of emotion, I sighed heavily. "I suppose there's nothing to do about it now."

"Well, I *am* sorry for putting you in that position, Ivy. I—"

"I know that you had to do your job. I just wasn't expecting all that. I suppose if my lawyer weren't my father, it wouldn't have been such an issue." I looked up into Luke's deep blue eyes and saw they were starting to sparkle. The smile on his face told me I'd let him off the hook a little too soon, so I added, "Then again, if you hadn't pulled me in for questioning in the first place, it wouldn't have been a problem at all."

"Ah, now, Ms. Ivy," the southern boy charm was oozing again, "I did ask you nicely, and it was on the weekend. If I'd been officially questioning you, I'd have waited until Monday morning, and that would have really set the grapevine on fire."

I suppressed a smile and shook my head at the ease with which he slipped into his flirting mode and nodded at the truth in his statement. "Speaking of the grapevine, I need to get moving. The longer we talk, the more people will want to know what we said. Besides, this little darling needs to go home to her mama." The pup was getting wriggly, the way Anna Claire gets when I've been chatting too long after church. "Anyway, consider yourself forgiven—mostly," I added as an afterthought. "And thanks for bringing me in to help out today."

"Yes, ma'am," Swaim drawled. "If there's anything else I can do, you just give me a holler."

I laughed as I walked away.

By the middle of the afternoon, many of the rescued animals had been reclaimed. The local news affiliate sent a camera crew out to cover the story, and while I did not want to be interviewed on camera, they did take a statement from me and filmed some of the footage against the backdrop of my lavender van. The guy sent to represent the newspaper caught me with his camera shortly after a large mutt of undetermined breeding had showered me with soap and water. I gave my permission for the photo to be used, because even with me drenched, the logo on my van was clearly visible, and the free advertising would do no harm.

I was just finishing up with my last dog when one of the PAWS staff came to get me. She didn't tell me why, other than to say I was needed on the phone. Of course, I immediately thought of Anna and checked to see if I'd missed a call on my cell. After I saw that it was clear, I realized neither Anna nor her grandparents would have known I was at PAWS. In spite of my confusion, I answered the phone professionally.

"Hi, this is Ivy. How can I help you?"

"Ivy! This is Chelsea Reed, Strawberry's mommy. I just wanted to thank you for your help. I have been so worried about Strawberry! I'm in Florida for Spring Break, and my neighbor was supposed to take care of her for me, but then she disappeared. I was going to come home to look for her, but Mrs. Jenson—she's my neighbor—said there had been some animal thefts. I knew there wasn't much I could do, so I just stayed here. I'll be home on Saturday, and I know Strawberry will be in great hands while she's with you. I work for your mom, you know? I'm her graduate assistant. She talks about you all the time, about how good you are with animals and that you live in the country and have chickens and all that, so I know my baby piggy will be happy with you until I get home."

There was more, but her words came in such a flurry they were hard to keep track of. Besides, I was distracted by the fact that she admitted to working for my mom. My mother is not easy to work for, and rarely refers to her grad students by name—they are usually "that boy" or "that girl" or "the stupid little twit," which is gender neutral and can apply to anyone at HDU—so I wouldn't have known Chelsea's name anyway. I couldn't remember saying I would watch someone's dog, but I didn't mind as long as it got along well with Baskin and Robin, didn't eat my shoes or my bird, and didn't poop on my floor. I was even amused by the idea that someone would name their dog Strawberry. But all my happy thoughts came to a screeching halt when I heard the words "baby piggy."

"Wait, what?" I stammered.

Chelsea kept talking like I hadn't made a sound. "If you have any questions, just Google miniature pigs, and you'll learn all sorts of good stuff. Pinnacle Pets has her food in stock. Don't worry, I'll pay you back next week. You can leave her food out for her and just fill the bowl up when it's empty. And she drinks regular water, you know, like from the tap? So don't worry about having to use filtered or bottled water; she isn't that sensitive. And it's okay to take her outside. She goes outside to potty, and I've taken her on walks and stuff, so she's seen grass before and knows what to do. And like I said, I'll be home Saturday—well, really, like Saturday night—and probably late now that I know Strawberry is okay, so I'll get in touch with you Sunday or Monday to collect her. Your mother knows how to get ahold of you, right? Do you think she'll get mad at me for calling her to get your number?"

My mouth moved, but no sound came out. It wouldn't have mattered. Chelsea's rapid-fire monologue would put an auctioneer to shame.

"She probably would, wouldn't she? Oh, but that's right! You have a dog-grooming business! I'll just look that up on Sunday, and I'll call you. You have a daughter, right? Strawberry loves kids, so everything will be great! Thanks so much! Bye!"

I managed to cough out "Uh-uh-uh," but Chelsea had already disconnected. I looked at the receiver in my hand, then at the volunteers at the desk who had been watching me, all of whom promptly ducked their heads and pretended to be on calls. The staff member who had come to fetch me had disappeared. I had no one to whom I could voice an objection.

I sighed and set the receiver back in its cradle, then went out to clean up my van before heading over to Pinnacle Pets for—what else?—pig food.

Before taking Strawberry home, you could have fit everything I knew about pigs into Tinkerbell's teacup. Pinnacle Pets did, indeed, have a bag of Strawberry's food on-hand—a forty-pound bag of premium, organic, miniature pig food, "the youth formula." It cost me almost fifty bucks. With my client base dwindling, I hoped Chelsea would reimburse me for the expense.

Once home, I carried Baskin into the house first. I was concerned about his emotional state and didn't want him to run away in fear. After settling him in Anna's bedroom with an ecstatic Robin, I returned to the van to collect Strawberry. Since I had no idea whether she was truly potty trained or not, I let her out on the screened porch. I had to admit she was a very cute little pig, with light pink skin and coarse white hair. Her delicate little hooves were a slightly darker pink, and she had the longest eyelashes I've ever seen. I mean, seriously, I was surprised my hair didn't move when she blinked. Chelsea hadn't told me the piglet's age, but I was guessing she was less than a year old because, well, she seemed "youthful."

Not trusting her to stay close once we were outside, I made Strawberry a harness from an old t-shirt and attached a leash to it. The piglet seemed happy to put her feet on grass. She made a grunt-squeal noise a couple of times before hopping around. I think it was the pig version of a happy dance. Snout to the ground, she led me on a meandering journey to the back fence, where she took care of her business. She went nose-to-tail-feather with several of the chickens, before escorting me on a brief but thorough inspection of the yard closest to the house. When we reached the back door again, Strawberry waited expectantly with her front hooves on the bottom step, looking between the door and me, until I picked her up and went inside.

Then it was time to eat.

Not knowing the correct amount to feed a piglet or how long it had been since she'd had a decent meal, I put half a cup of her food in an old bowl and set it on the floor for her. If you think about it, pigs aren't built for cute movements like wiggling, but Strawberry managed to carry off that very act with the help of her flapping ears and flat little tail. While she ate, she made adorable grunting and snuffling noises. She was just so cute I almost forgot to leave her alone so I could do some research.

In the short period of time I had between feeding Ebony and hearing Strawberry's protests over being locked in another room, I discovered that miniature pigs were supposed to be smart, easily trained, and not given to craving affection—more like a cat than a dog. During my brief exposure to this particular porker, I could check off items one and two, but I really thought Strawberry missed the memo on not needing a lot of attention. Then again, I didn't know how long she'd been held captive, so maybe she was just feeling insecure. I quickly learned that the half-cup portion of food I'd given her was less than what she should have been served based on weight. Strawberry was as tall, but not as long as Robin, and when I carried her up my back steps, I'd guessed she weighed less than twenty pounds. Based on my limited research, I was also able to estimate her age at around six months.

Strawberry was, indeed, a baby pig.

I introduced her to Ebony the same way I would have introduced him to a new dog. I sat on the floor and made sure Strawberry was content and stationary, then I asked my bird to join us. Ebs has been around dogs his entire life, so he knew this new four-legged creature was not canine. He first sat on my head and hissed, trying to get a rise out of the piglet that was pressed up against my leg getting a belly rub. He slowly moved closer and closer until he was on the floor in front of the piggy, carefully eyeing her dainty pink hooves. When Strawberry rolled to her feet, Ebony backed up a step or two and raised his crest feathers, but otherwise held his ground. The curious little sow extended her snout to give him an investigatory sniff, then looked at me as if to ask what she was allowed to do next. I kept my hand on her, gently stroking her back until I was sure the two animals were comfortable with each other.

Finally, Ebony relaxed his crest, fluffed out every feather on his body, cocked his head, and said, "Ivory?"

Chapter 19

When I answered my phone on Wednesday evening, I was stifling a yawn. Anna's greeting sounded like she was doing the same.

"Hi, Mama! Guess what we did today?"

Anna sounded a little less enthusiastic than she had on our previous calls. I wondered if her day had been less exciting than the last few or if she was merely tired.

"Did you fly again?"

"No, but we floated."

"Floated? Like on a magic carpet or a cloud?"

My baby's laugh was like music to my ears.

"No, Mama, not today. We went swimming!"

"Swimming? It's only March." Typically, in Texas, the only swimming one does in March is incidental, when, in a moment of stupidity, you forget that your purple work vehicle is not, in fact, amphibious and will not allow you to cross flooded roads without getting soaked. (Again, don't ask.) I know there are people who have indoor pools, or heated outdoor pools, but I'm not acquainted with any of them.

"Yes!" Her voice reflected how amazed she was by

this act. "And we were outside!"

"Was the water cold?"

"Well, it was hot, so the water felt really good, but we went to a water park, and one place looked like it had snow everywhere."

"Really? Why?"

"Because it was called Buzzard Beach and . . ." She paused to listen to someone in the background. She giggled and told whoever it was, "Oh! That makes sense! I didn't think buzzards liked snow."

Her attention turned back to me. "It was called *Blizzard* Beach. You know, kind of like the ice cream we get at Dairy Queen?" In a whisper, she added, "I thought it was called Buzzard Beach, and I kept looking for them all day but didn't see any. Now I know why!"

I laughed. I couldn't wait for my baby to get home. "So, there was snow near the water?"

"Not real snow, but it looked like it. There were all these water slides, and they were like blue tubes—but not dark blue—and the snow stuff looked like it was way above our heads! There was some snow on a rock near the water. I touched it, but it didn't feel like the snow we got at home that one time. Maybe it snows differently here. There was this slide we went down that was really big and wide, and looked like it was made of ice!"

"Did that make the water cold?"

Anna's initial response was to give me the *Oh-Mama-you're-so-goofy* laugh.

"I didn't think so, but Grandmom said it was too chilly for her. She didn't go down any of the slides or get in the pool with the waves, but she did take me around on a big float. It was supposed to be on a river, but it was just pool water going in a long path."

"How do you know that?"

"Because we floated past people who were doing things like going to the snack bar and sitting out in the sun, but mostly it was because the water was clear and not brown and muddy like it is at home."

A memory flashed in my mind of Anna at about four years old, coloring a river brown in her coloring book and stating that she'd never seen a blue river before because all of ours had mud.

"Is it more fun to float in clear water?"

"I don't know. Maybe. It was fun to look down and see the bottom."

"So, were you at the water park all day?"

"Uh-huh, but we didn't just get in the water . . ."

I'm a terrible mother. My only child had spent the last few nights telling me enough about her trip to Disney World that I should have felt like I had been there, too, but I hadn't been listening to a lot of it. I had been dwelling on the deeds of evil people and imagining horrible scenarios involving animals that I love. Now that all the stolen animals were safe, I still wasn't giving Anna all of my attention. Instead, I was trying to decide how best to bed down a guest piglet.

The absence of Anna's voice over the airwaves alerted me that a response was needed.

"Oh, that sounds like fun."

"It was, and guess who we saw—Lilo and Stitch! In the movie, they look like they would be little, but they were really big."

"So, were they bigger than me?"

"Well, yeah." This was said with the innocent practicality of a child. "Stitch was about as tall as Aunt

Gina, but not as tall as Uncle Jace. And Lilo was pretty. Do you think all the girls at Disney are pretty?"

"I think they're supposed to look pretty when they're at the park, but at home, they probably look like normal people."

"Kind of like how you look prettier when you get dressed up to go to church than when you go outside to work in the garden?"

"Exactly." I was glad that Anna thought I looked nice at least some of the time and that she could tell the difference between my church and yardwork attires.

"I guess princesses are people, too, huh?"

"You bet. Being a princess is a job."

"Like the judge at court is a job."

"Right." It was good to know she'd remembered something of our last conversation. "Did you go anywhere else today?"

"No, we stayed at the water park. I guess it was really two water parks. At the second one, the one with the boat, there was this waterfall we got to float under. Granddaddy tried to act like he was mad that we got him wet, but he wasn't. He laughed."

"It sounds like you had a lot of fun."

"We did. Grandmom and Aunt Gina kept putting sunblock on everybody, so we didn't get burned or anything. Grandmom said she was more worried about the sun bouncing off the snow and onto us, so we went to that park early."

After a moment I realized that for the third day in a row Anna hadn't called the Greenes "Grandmother" or "Grandfather." The "Grandmom" and "Granddaddy" thing was sticking.

Anna yawned, spawning another from me.

"It was a good day," she said, "but we have to leave tomorrow."

"Where are you going tomorrow?"

Again, the laugh. "I get to come back to Texas! Does that mean I get to see you tomorrow?"

I smiled. "Yes, baby, it does! Are you happy about that?"

"I think so. It was a lot of fun here, but I miss you. I miss Ebony, and Baskin and Robin, too."

"Well, all of us have missed you. Robin told me she can't wait for you to come home and sleep with her again."

Anna giggled. "She did not! Robin doesn't talk."

"Okay, maybe she didn't say it in words, but I can tell she was thinking it."

About that time, Strawberry squealed, letting me know she didn't like being stuck on the floor by herself.

"What was that noise?"

I had to think fast. Fortunately, the bird in my lap gave me an idea. "Umm . . . Ebony seems to be learning a new sound. I haven't figured out what it is yet."

That must have satisfied her curiosity, because she promptly changed the subject. "Mama, I watched a lot of people today, but I tried not to think about doing things better than them. There was one lady who fell down in the wave pool. I didn't laugh because I wouldn't want someone to laugh at me if I fell down."

"That's sweet of you, Anna Claire. You're a good person."

"I thought about that Bible sentence a lot today. I think it's because I slept good last night."

"Do you think you'll sleep well tonight?"

"I don't know. I'm really tired, but I'm also excited

that I get to see you tomorrow." She paused, sighed—or yawned—and asked, "Do you have another Bible piece for me tonight?"

"I do! This one is from Philippians."

"What are Philippians? Are they a funny color like the people at Avatar?"

"I'm not really sure, but I think they're a group of people who lived when Jesus lived," I answered. "They would have looked a lot like the people Jesus knew, and probably weren't blue."

"Okay, good," she said, sounding genuinely relieved.

"So, this sentence is from a letter the apostle Paul wrote to the Philippians. It says, 'I can do all things through Him who gives me strength.' It means that when God and Jesus are on your side, you can do anything or be anything."

"Like fly?"

"Well, maybe. You would have to have absolutely, positively, no doubt at all that God wanted you to fly." I was beginning to question my own judgment on this verse. The last thing I wanted was for Anna to decide that God wanted her to fly and actually try it. Maybe He would make it possible, but then again, maybe my own grown-up doubts would weigh her down.

"Didn't Jesus walk on water?"

"He did."

"Was it because He knew God wanted Him to?"

"I'm sure that was part of it, but it was also because He was the Son of God."

"Being the Son of God gave Him special powers, huh?"

"I guess so."

"I think that's a lot to think about tonight. Is it okay if I think about it tomorrow?"

"Of course, baby. You have plenty of time."

"I love you, Mama. I can't wait to see you."

Chapter 20

You would think that after a restless night on Tuesday and then bathing almost a dozen dogs, I would have been tired enough Wednesday night to sleep like a rock. Unfortunately, much as I wanted to enter the land of slumber, it wasn't meant to be.

The first hurdle between me and sleep was Strawberry. Although she appeared to be housebroken, I wasn't keen on the idea of letting her have the run of the house just to find pig poop all over my floors in the morning. I initially thought about housing her on the back porch, but with a brisk northerly wind blowing, I didn't want her to get cold. The sunroom seemed like an ideal spot, but it turns out that Strawberry is clearly a very spoiled little pig who hates to be left alone. I ended up making her a play area in the corner of my bedroom, using an old sheet stretched between two small tables for the wall that had to be erected, and old blankets and towels for her bed. She rooted, grunted, and generally made a semi-quiet nuisance of herself for a lot longer than I expected.

The second issue was that, while my body was

tired, my mind was full of highly animated thoughts in anticipation of Anna's return. This kind of thing is rare for me as an adult, but my baby had been gone for five days—FIVE DAYS!—and it seemed like she'd literally been gone FOR*EVER*! I had missed her smile, her sweet voice as she talked to the animals, and, well, everything about her. I could not wait to hold her for as long as she'd allow.

I don't know what time it was when I finally dozed off, but I can honestly say that when my internal alarm clock woke me at 5:00 a.m., I was less than happy. Robin had deserted me sometime during the night, probably because I'd been so restless. I got up and padded to the bathroom in the dark before returning to switch on the light in search of clothing. Ebony's cage gets covered by a blanket every night, so the light doesn't bother him in the morning. I did, however, forget about Strawberry. When the overhead light came on, that little girl squealed like . . . well, she squealed like a petulant pig, jolting me out of whatever sleep had followed me out of bed and startling Ebony enough that he flapped around in his cage.

I immediately turned the light off again and felt around for a lamp with less intrusive brightness. After checking to be sure Ebony was in one piece, I peeked into Strawberry's improvised pen and found her snuggled up next to Robin. Both dog and piglet were giving me the stink eye and trust me when I say you have not received a dirty look until you've gotten one from a rudely awakened oinker. I left them alone and went in search of a bathrobe and some good, strong tea.

I didn't have to be at Chip's to meet the Greenes until noon, but I also didn't want a replay of last

Sunday's mad dash to church. I got myself showered and dressed, then set about finding a location for a suitable pen for Strawberry. She'd gone through the night without any accidents, but I didn't want to come home and have to clean up a mess. The best place seemed to be my garage, so I pulled the pickup out into the driveway, then used an old drop cloth as a barrier across the building's opening. Inside, I made sure the floor was free of contaminants before I set up a portable dog pen. My thinking was that by utilizing the garage, Strawberry could have some fresh air for the day without being exposed to the elements, and if she figured out a way to get out of the pen, the barrier would serve as a failsafe. Even more than not wanting to come home to a room full of piglet poop, I didn't want to have to search for a wandering swine.

Just to be on the safe side, I wrote my name and phone number on a piece of red ribbon and tied it around Strawberry's neck and shoulders.

With all my animals fed, and Ebony properly cuddled prior to yet another day of being left alone, I was ready to go by nine. You would think that having three hours to make a seventy-minute drive would make me happy, but I still felt like I was behind schedule. I left the house and drove into town to gas up and grab a bite to eat. I left the pump running for the pickup and went into the store to see what they had left over from their early breakfast rush. Armed with a freshly assembled spicy-egg-and-cheese kolache and a bottled Dr Pepper, I finally felt ready to go pick up my baby.

I really should have known better than to "feel ready" for anything, ever. Just as I was about to climb in the truck, I saw Daryl walking up the street. He looked like any other wanderer, with a backpack on his shoulders and a duffle bag slung across his chest. He was also, much to my relief, fully clothed in jeans, a t-shirt, and an unzipped jacket. My issue here was that Daryl had assured me he would be on a bus out of town before the end of the week, but here he was walking north, and the bus station is on the southern end of town. Much as I told myself to mind my own business and let him be on his way, I just couldn't help myself. Instead, I cranked up the pickup and went after him.

"Hey," I said, startling him as I pulled up next to him. The poor guy looked so relieved to see it was me that I almost felt bad for being suspicious of him.

"Oh, hi, Ivy. I almost didn't recognize you without your camper."

"Are you on your way out of town?" I studied his face when I asked this, looking for signs of guilt or deception.

Daryl nodded. "Yep, just like I promised."

"You do know the bus station is in the other direction, right?"

He nodded again. "I dropped a whole bunch of dishes the other day at work and had to pay for them, so my last check was really small. If I paid for a bus ticket, I wouldn't have any money to eat on until I get a new job. I figured I'd get to the edge of town and try to bum a ride from a trucker or something."

Now I did feel bad for my suspicions.

"Where are you going today?" he asked.

"I'm on my way to a little place near Terrell to meet my in-laws and pick up my daughter." Daryl gave me a blank look, and it occurred to me that since he wasn't from here, he probably hadn't heard of Terrell, Texas.

To clarify, I said, "It's a small city just outside of Dallas."

"Hey, I bet Dallas would be a good place for me to get a job. I always secretly liked the Cowboys, too. Do you mind if I ride along with you?"

I hesitated. I honestly didn't think Daryl was dangerous by any stretch of the imagination, but I wasn't sure I wanted to spend more than an hour in a small space with him. He *was* wearing standard blue jeans—and not tear-away pants—but on the other hand, I didn't know if he was the kind of person to go days without showering.

"I can even ride in the bed of the truck," he offered hopefully. "I don't mind being a little cold."

I sighed and said, "No, you can ride up front. Get in."

I glanced around as he made his way to the passenger door, hoping no one was watching and that I wouldn't have to answer questions later about the stranger climbing in my pickup. Putting my paranoia aside, I reasoned that the chances of anyone noticing the simple act of a young man getting into my van were slim at best.

Fortunately, Daryl did not exude the scent of the unwashed; instead, as the aroma of cheese, bread, and jalapeno quickly saturated the air, I heard his stomach growling loud enough to intimidate a grizzly. Since he had admitted to pinching his pennies, I guessed that he hadn't eaten before getting on the road. I, however, had inhaled a couple of pieces of toast with my tea. With a sigh, I handed him the kolache but retained possession of the Dr Pepper. A girl has to have her limits.

"Thanks! I'm starving," he said between mouthfuls.

"Hey, I saw you on TV last night. The news said they caught the guys that were stealing the animals. So my map . . . did it help?"

I nodded. "Your map was great. My friend James and I went out there on Tuesday afternoon to check it out, then we called the police. The detective who helped us said we caught them just before they moved all the animals out."

"That's a relief! So everybody got their dog back?"

"There were more than just dogs," I answered, giving him a rundown of the counts I remembered from the day before. "By the time I left the PAWS facility yesterday, there were only a few animals who couldn't be matched with an owner. If those people don't come forward after seeing the news, those animals will be adopted out to new homes."

I couldn't think of anything more to add, so I turned my attention to the road in front of us.

"So," Daryl said around a mouthful of food a few moments later, "tell me about your daughter."

I'm not big on making small talk, so I generally save it for my customers. Besides, he was a flasher who liked to dress up for holidays—I didn't want to share any information that might make him want to hang around until after Easter. I don't know what expression I was wearing, but it couldn't have been a pleasant one because he swallowed audibly and looked out the window. A few minutes after finishing off his—*my*—breakfast, Daryl slumped down in the seat and went to sleep.

The radio was playing low, providing little more than a background accompaniment to road noise, and the combination of the two gave my mind a great excuse to wander. The first place it lingered was on the subject of Anna's new labels for Rex's parents. I certainly didn't mind that she'd begun to refer to them as "Grandmom" and "Granddaddy," but it seemed a little sudden. On the other hand, she had just spent the better part of four days with them at the Magic Kingdom, and they likely had a whole new relationship. Still, I couldn't help but consider that Anna had spent volumes more time with my parents—though not all at once—and she still addressed them with the more formal titles of "Grandmother" and "Grandfather." As often as she sees my parents, I would think she'd want to have more casual names for them, too. I honestly had no idea and decided I would bring it up with Anna when the time seemed right.

I sent my thoughts off in another direction, where they settled upon the subject of Strawberry. That was going to be a delicate situation once Anna was home. I had no doubt she would instantly fall in love with the piglet, and I wondered how long it would take before my daughter stopped asking me to buy her a pig. At the same time, it was possible that the oinker would take her mind off the more realistic request for a kitten. I didn't want to get her a kitten any more than I wanted to add a pig to our household, but at least a cat had the potential for earning its keep by catching mice and other garage- and henhouse-dwelling rodents. A pig would just eat until it wasn't cute any longer, and it wasn't like we could harvest bacon from a former family pet.

Daryl made an odd noise and shifted, then went straight back to sleep. That disruption was enough to take my mind off pork and send it in search of another topic to ponder—pet-napping. What kind of person steals another person's fur-baby? I could almost understand if it were a case of coveting said pet and not having the resources to acquire one legally, but really, even that scenario didn't make sense. Taking a large volume of other people's pets—especially if you had to break into their homes—completely boggled my mind. I hadn't asked if other valuables were stolen, but I'm sure I would have remembered hearing something about it on the news. As it was, there had been no mention of the theft of other items that could be easily resold or pawned. I have never understood why people hurt others for fun or profit. Meanness for meanness' sake is senseless in my opinion.

That brought me to my biggest concern: what would now happen to my business? I was confident that once the dust settled on this pet-related crime my business would pick up again. My loyal customers would stay with me and would likely continue to provide favorable recommendations. Those who would forever be suspicious of me would probably have found an excuse to cut me loose anyway. It was the people on the fence—those who weren't in such a hurry to condemn me but were also wary when it came to the wellbeing of their canine babies—that bothered me. I wasn't sure what I could do to convince them that I hadn't been involved in this latest incident and didn't know if I should even try. My business had enjoyed a short-term boost months ago, right after I got mixed up in the aforementioned murder investigation. Only one or two of those people were still clients. The rest had called for a one-time visit so they could try to get the juicy details out of me before their friends did. I knew there would likely be a similar scenario in the coming week or two, now that the pet thieves had been caught. Unfortunately, there wasn't a good way to identify these gossipmongers until they showed their true colors. A brief boost in business would be nice, though, especially if it helped defray my losses of the last few days. After that, I would have to do some creative marketing to try to draw in new customers.

My schedule for the remainder of the week was open. I had known about Anna's Spring Break trip since January and had been able to adjust my appointments accordingly. Still, given the lust for information craved by the previously mentioned gossip hounds, I was surprised I hadn't received at least one call or text. I glanced over at the phone cradle mounted to the dashboard. It was empty, which sent a burst of adrenaline rocketing through my system. Coincidentally, Daryl woke up at that same moment, yawning loudly and stretching.

"What did you do with my phone?" I was nearly shouting.

"Huh?" Apparently, Daryl isn't very sharp when he first awakens (not that I have any room to talk).

"My phone? What did you do with it? If you give it back now, I won't be mad." Ha! I would be of course, but at least I wouldn't be panicked, too.

"I don't have your phone." He looked alarmed and innocent all at the same time.

I began looking around on the floor of the truck and trying to see into the dark spaces beneath me.

"Look on your side," I instructed. "And look in the back seat."

As instructed, Daryl searched his side of the cab

while I pulled to the shoulder of the road. I got out to check the bed of the pickup, then hunted around on my side of the backseat while Daryl looked around on the passenger side. When we both came up empty, I glared at him.

"I promise you, Ivy, I don't have your phone!" He pushed his bags in my direction. "Feel free to search my stuff. I don't have it."

I was tempted to dump the contents of his pack and his duffle in the bed of the truck, but that kind of privacy invasion isn't in my DNA, especially when I believed him when he said he was innocent.

"Maybe you left it at the gas station," he suggested.

I sighed while I searched my peanut-sized memory for any recollection of the cell and the convenience store. As an afterthought, I patted my pockets. There it was, tucked snugly into my back pocket.

"Ha ha," Daryl laughed. "That's what you get for accusing people of things."

I was so relieved to find it that my knees almost buckled. I apologized to my passenger, then checked for any new notifications. The only thing I saw were the words "No Service."

We both climbed back into the truck, where I apologized again before putting my phone in the cradle and pulling back out onto the interstate. Daryl was quiet for a few moments, but his buoyant personality wasn't one to be bogged down for long.

"You know what you could do to make it up to me?" he asked. When my answer was nothing more than a glance in his direction, he said, "How about you ask your in-laws to give me a ride?"

Now it was my turn to laugh.

"Why is that funny?" Daryl looked offended by my amusement.

"It's a long story," I answered. "And complicated. Let's just leave it as a firm *No*."

"Ah, come on, tell me. We have a little time . . . don't we?"

I saw the sign stating the first exit for Terrell was just a mile away. I nailed my passenger with my meanest glare and said, "You have two choices. You can ask me again, and I'll put you out here, or you can drop it, and I'll take you into the next town and let you out somewhere that might get you a decent ride."

He hesitated, but only for a second. "How far is the next town?"

I had more than enough time to go ten miles out of my way to ensure Daryl wouldn't wander up and introduce himself to the Greenes while I was welcoming my baby girl home. I listened with half an ear as he yammered on about all the jobs he thought would be available to him in Dallas. It wasn't long before I was turning into a parking lot on the corner of the two main roads through Terrell. There was a fast food chain on site across the parking lot from a strip mall and a tire store.

"Thanks for the ride, Ivy," Daryl said as he opened his door. "And thanks for not outing me to the cops about my dancing."

"Thank you, Daryl, for your map. You really helped a lot of people by telling me where to find all those animals."

He smiled a huge, toothy smile, and I got an instant mental picture of what he'd looked like as a mischievous yet good-hearted little boy.

"Can I give you a little advice?" I asked. When he nodded, I said, "Dallas is a huge city. Don't spend all your free time looking for little old ladies to . . . dance for. Get a job, save some money, and put your dancing pants away for a while."

His grin dimmed but didn't disappear completely. "Thanks again, Ivy."

I shook my head in bewilderment as my leprechaun acquaintance/fellow pet-napper sleuth wandered off across the parking lot.

Chapter 21

I was the first to arrive at Chip's. With butterflies fluttering in my stomach and my head swarming with the crazy events of recent days, I had no desire to sit in my truck and wait. Even though Anna and I had spoken on the phone each night she was gone, it was hard for me to quantify, even to myself, how much I'd missed my baby. I felt like Anna had her own light, and without it, my world felt dark.

In hopes of distracting myself, I checked my phone for messages. There were none. Instinctively, I looked in the rearview mirror. At the same instant that my eyes caught sight of the entrance, the Greenes' SUV turned into the parking lot. In that briefest moment, everything around me seemed brighter and happier.

I slid out of the pickup and waited for them to choose a parking spot before I started in their direction. Mr. Greene didn't see me at first because he'd driven to the other side of the lot. I resisted the urge to jump up and down and wave my arms. When the SUV finally came to a stop, it was across a grassy expanse that seemed to grow larger as I stepped onto it. In a blink, the back door flew open, and Anna was racing across the lawn to meet me. With the force of a runaway train, she slammed into me, wrapping her arms around my legs. I lifted her up and we spun around, holding tight to one another. My baby girl giggled and squealed as we moved, her vocalizations like music to my ears.

When I set her down and stepped back half a pace, I realized one thing instantly: Anna had grown at least a foot taller. I barely had to bend over to look her in the eyes. The idea that my little daughter was growing up too quickly wasn't even enough to dim the joy I felt at seeing her.

"Oh, Mama, I have so much to tell you!"

"Anna, you got so big!"

We spoke at the same time, laughing at each other and coming together for another hug.

"I missed you, baby," I muttered into the top of her head as I planted a kiss in her hair.

"I have a surprise for you!" she squealed as she wriggled out from my arms. "I brought you a *real* Florida orange! They gave us one on the plane, and I almost ate mine, but I wanted to save it and share it with you."

What happened next was so out of the blue and unprecedented, I half-expected the leprechaun to poke his lurid red head out from behind the tree and exclaim, "Surprise!" Before I could so much as thank my dear girl for her gift, Rex's mom gathered me into a heartfelt embrace. I was so shocked I almost forgot to hug her back.

"Oh, Ivy, we had such a good time with Anna," she said. "She is such a delight."

"Thank you." The words that fell from my mouth

were sincere, but the sudden display of affection was so unexpected that I wasn't sure it had actually been me saying them. Next to me, Anna squirmed with a mixture of pleasure and embarrassment and reached for my hand.

"I wish I could bottle this little girl's energy," Mr. Greene said as he touched the tip of her nose affectionately.

I nodded, desperately searching for a suitable reply. Finally, I managed to say, "I know what you mean. Some days I have trouble keeping up with her."

Anna looked up at me, rolled her eyes, and said, "Oh, Mama, you do not."

We adults chuckled in unison.

Sensing the Greenes had something more to say, I gently squeezed my daughter's hand and said, "Anna Claire, why don't you go put your suitcase in the truck. It's unlocked."

She grinned, apparently pleased to have an excuse to get out of the spotlight. She took the valise from her grandfather, striding away from us like a girl on a mission. If purpose and maturity could be demonstrated by a gait, Anna was showing off both.

I felt my face glow with pride as I watched her.

"We appreciate you letting us take her this week," Mr. Greene said. "She always behaves well when she's with us, but this time she really seemed to come out of her shell."

"Oh, my, yes," Mrs. Greene agreed. "Everything seemed a little tense that first night she was with us, but once she knew we were going somewhere on a plane with her cousin, Anna positively blossomed!"

"She loves to go places," I said, before adding, "I

hope she didn't talk your ear off too many times."

"No, no, not at all." Mrs. Greene beamed in the direction of my baby.

"She's a very observant little girl," Mr. Greene commented. "And she seems to know about a great many things."

"She loves school," I supplied, "and learning."

Rex's mother gathered me in for another hug as Anna approached us. "Thank you so much for letting her come with us. I know it couldn't have been easy for you." She paused, then seemed to regain her resolve. "We would love if you could accompany us one of these times."

I was dumbfounded. Here was a lady who usually made a fairy tale ice queen look like Cupid's apprentice, only now she was gushing with genuine warmth. All I could do was nod.

Once Mrs. Greene released me, Mr. Greene stepped forward and took my hand in both of his. "You're doing a fine job of raising a remarkable young lady, Ivy. We're thankful she's our granddaughter, and I know Rex would be proud."

Once we said our goodbyes, and Anna was securely settled into her car seat, we got back on the road. I was trying to decide which subject to broach: that of her new names for her grandparents or the fact that we had a pig waiting for us at home. I was very curious about the former, but I also didn't want to make a big deal out of it. As for the latter, well, I just didn't even want to get into *that* before I had to.

"Grandmom said you knew we were going to Disney World the whole time," Anna said with just a hint of accusation in her voice.

"I did," I admitted. "It was supposed to be a surprise."

"Oh, it was!"

"Was it a good surprise?" I already knew the answer, but I had to ask.

"Oh, yes! It was one of the best surprises of my whole life!"

I had to chuckle at that statement. I couldn't imagine a more delightful gift for a six-year-old than a Magic Kingdom vacation—unless it was a pony, or perhaps a pig.

"I thought about my homework every day, but I don't remember what the exact words were. I know one was confusing, one was about judges, and one came from the Philip people, but that's about all." With a serious look on her face, Anna added, "You read them to me, and I said them back to you, but I've slept since then."

I laughed outright and wondered where my daughter had heard that expression. Fortunately, in the time I'd had earlier in the day, I'd written the verses on oversized recipe cards. I took them down from the visor where I'd tucked them away when I left the house and handed them over the seat to Anna.

"I wrote them down for you, baby," I said. "You know, in case you forgot something in your sleep."

Anna giggled and took the cards from my hand.

"Okay, so the confusing one is first. 'Now faith is confidence in what we hope for and assurance for what we do not see.'" Anna stumbled a little on the word "confidence," so I helped her out with "assurance." "That's the one where we know God is there even though we can't look at His face, right?"

"Right. Confidence means you believe in something, and an assurance is like a promise."

"Okay," she replied, nodding. "The next one is, 'I can do all things through Him who gives me strength.' That's the one that means if God is on my side I can do anything."

"Correct."

"And the last one is the judge one. 'Judge not, that ye not be judged.' What's a 'ye'?"

"That means the same as the word 'you.' It's the way people talked a long time ago," I answered.

"Oh. That's kind of weird, don't you think?"

"I guess. If people from that time were here now, they'd probably think we were pretty weird, too."

Anna nodded and continued to study the card in her hands. Then she asked, "This is the one where we have to not talk bad about people, right?"

"Sort of. If you judge someone, you usually think that whatever they're doing is wrong and that you are a better person than they are."

"Like just now when you said people from a long time ago would think we're weird? Would they be judging us?"

"I think so. But remember, you thought they were weird first."

"So, it's okay to judge someone if they judge you first?"

"No, and that isn't what I said." I waited, hoping she would catch on to what I was trying to get her to understand.

The light that appeared when she caught on was almost blinding. "Oh, I get it! When I said they were weird, I was thinking the way I talk is better than how they talked."

"Exactly. And just because it's different . . ." I let my sentence trail off, again hoping Anna would pick it up.

"Being different isn't better or worse—it's just different," she stated with certainty.

"Very good, Anna Claire. Can you think of another example of someone judging someone else?"

She thought for a moment, turning her head to gaze out the window. "What about when Timmy Anders says chocolate milk is better than regular milk?"

Ah, Timmy Anders, I thought. Anna's classmate and nemesis—the boy who seems to be at the root of all the mischief at Pinnacle Christian Academy. I should have expected he would come up as an example.

"That's pretty close, but since milk doesn't have feelings, it doesn't really work for this Bible passage."

"Oh." That single, short word was full of disappointment and uncertainty. "This is hard. Can you tell me one more?"

I nodded, sure that an idea would pop in my head that would be a perfect illustration of the dangers of being judgmental. My words failed me, though, and I had to admit that it wasn't an easy task when the spotlight was pointed at me. Anna waited patiently while I sifted through thoughts and memories. The only things that came to mind were the fingers of people pointing at me all week, and how much I didn't like it, and then me accusing Daryl of taking my phone. My response began to take shape.

"Okay, baby girl, try this. Pretend for a minute you're at the grocery store looking for something—"

"Like cereal?"

"Okay, that works. You're in the grocery store trying to decide on the kind of cereal you want, and some lady you've never seen before comes up with the store manager and says that she saw you take a candy bar and put it in your pocket."

"But I wouldn't do that!" Anna protested.

"I know that, and you know that, but say this lady doesn't like kids."

"And that's why she thinks I did something wrong? Just because I'm a kid?"

"Uh-huh," I answered, nodding. "What do you think about that?"

"That's not fair!"

"You're right; it isn't fair. What do you think it is when someone thinks you did something bad just because of who you are?"

"She would be judging me, wouldn't she?"

"That's exactly right."

"So, what's the 'lest ye be judged' part, then?"

I started to answer, but I wanted to see if Anna could come up with something on her own. "You think about it and tell me."

"Okay." She smiled, growing excited by the idea of the challenge. The cab of the truck was quiet while she worked out a response. "What if someone told the manager the lady stole money?"

"Why would they do that?"

"Maybe it's because they don't like her shoes. Maybe the lady is wearing brown shoes and this person doesn't like the color brown, so they try to get her in trouble. Would that be judging her?"

I couldn't hold back my smile of pride.

"Yes, baby, I think that would be an example of

judging her."

"So what God wants us to know is that judging people is bad, and it makes them feel bad, and if they do it back to us, it'll make *us* feel bad, and none of that is good, right?"

I thought about that for a moment. Following along with Anna's reasoning was a little like trying to turn a wadded-up clump of string into a neat ball—you first had to find where it all began. She was right, but still was just missing the point. Since I wasn't sure how to explain it more clearly, I decided to leave it alone for the moment.

"Is that the Bible verse you want to use for your class?" I asked.

"I think so," she replied.

"Well, maybe Mrs. Danford can help you understand what God wants us to know."

"And then I can help you understand?" she suggested.

"Absolutely," I admitted. "I can always use help understanding things better."

Anna nodded happily and turned her attention to the scenery as we passed by. While we were talking, we'd turned off the interstate and now were less than thirty miles from home. I knew I would have to bring up the subject of Strawberry before we got to the house and decided that now was as good a time as any other.

"Anna, one of your grandmother's—my mother's— graduate students left her pet for us to take care of until she gets home," I began.

"Okay," she answered, as though she didn't have a care in the world.

"It's kind of an unusual pet," I added.

"Really? Like what? Should I guess?"

Maybe this would be easier than I thought.

"Sure, go ahead."

"Oh, good! Grandmom and Granddaddy liked to play this game with us. I get to ask you three questions about it before I answer—that way I'll have a better chance of being right. And I get three guesses."

I nodded my consent. Anna proceeded to ask about the number of legs on the animal, whether it had fur or feathers, and if it made noise. At first, I was a little concerned that she knew what it was, but when she wasn't specific about the sound Strawberry made, it was clear she didn't have a clue. Between each incorrect guess, my girl asked three more questions, narrowing the possibilities down from just about any living thing one could imagine, to animals she had seen on her trip. We had reached our road by the time she was out of guesses, and we were both laughing at her outrageous ideas.

"If it isn't a kangaroo, I don't know what it could be!" Anna flipped her hands in the air as she finished her sentence.

"It is definitely *not* a kangaroo," I answered. "Her name is Strawberry, and—"

"Strawberry?"

"Yes, and Strawberry is a pig."

"A *pig*? No way!"

I honestly don't know who squealed louder when we got home—my daughter or the piglet. Needless to say, it was love at first sight for both of them.

Anna immediately took over the oinker's care, using the leash to drag her around as she greeted Baskin, Robin, Ebony, and each of the chickens individually. Since Strawberry's tail never stopped twitching, I had to assume she didn't mind one bit.

Chapter 22

"No, I will not have my child sleeping with a pig!"

As a parent, there are times when you say and do things you never imagined, even in your wildest dreams. This wasn't the first such instance for me, and I knew it was far from the last, but still, deep inside, I cringed at these words. I prayed that I would never, ever, utter that specific combination of words again.

"But—" Anna's protest was cut short by a knock at my door.

I knew we would have at least one argument over Strawberry, but I didn't expect it would occur at bedtime or that it would be over the piggy's sleeping arrangements. Five days of excitement had finally caught up with Anna, and the closer we got to bedtime, the more obstinate she became—and over ridiculous things! She wanted to argue over the amount of toothpaste that should be used when brushing her teeth. She won that debate, but only because we couldn't put the excess toothpaste back in the tube. Just before that, she'd laid out a convincing case for moving Strawberry's makeshift sleeping quarters from my room to hers. (It had to do with Strawberry's instant attachment to Anna, and the fact that both girls—human and oinker—were happier with Robin close by.) If I were keeping score, then my daughter was winning the battle of wills two-to-one. My single victory was her 8:00 p.m. bedtime, and I'd only gotten her to comply because she'd yawned in the middle of her objection.

A second knock echoed through the house. Before going to answer the door, I scooped Strawberry up from the floor next to the bed and deposited her on her relocated pallet. Anna flopped back on her bed with an exaggerated sigh and shot me a dirty look before I switched off the light.

"Good night, baby girl," I said. "Sleep well."

I opened the door just as Detective Swaim was raising his hand to knock again. He'd called me earlier to say that he had an update for me on the animal theft case and that he had something to give me. I'd told him that was fine, and so I wasn't surprised to see him on my doorstep. I knew my mother would say that eight o'clock in the evening was too late for a visitor, but she wasn't here, and I didn't have any neighbors who would tell on me. Besides, I was curious about both the results of his investigation and about whatever he might be bringing me.

"Who's at the door, Mama?" Anna called out from the next room.

"Go to sleep, Anna Claire!" I answered. "If you're still awake when I come back in there, Strawberry will be sleeping in the henhouse tonight."

I heard her grumble something, but I couldn't make out the words.

"Good evening, Detective Swaim," I said, offering my visitor a smile.

"Aw, Ms. Ivy, this isn't an official visit. You can call me Luke." His southern gentleman charm was oozing in my direction as he pulled open my screen door. "Would you rather we talked out here? It's a lovely evening."

The breeze was out of the south, so the evening was mild and comfortable. I knew if we sat inside, Anna would either strain her ears trying to hear us or she'd get out of bed to join the conversation. I didn't see any reason for her to get involved in what had occurred while she was away, so I stepped out onto the porch and pulled the door closed behind me.

Luke ushered me to the chair closest to the door, which meant he would have to look into the light for the duration of our conversation. I appreciated the consideration. Still unnerved from his recent abduction, Baskin hovered at the edge of the porch light's glow, growling.

"I know you've been waiting to hear what we found out from the two men we picked up yesterday morning," Swaim began as he perched on the front edge of the chair. "Both have long histories with law enforcement, and the man who is the apparent ringleader is a pretty tough customer. He immediately asked for a lawyer and wouldn't tell us a thing. The other guy is no angel either, but he was at least happy to give us the details of their operation. As we suspected, they were going to start moving the animals yesterday. Some were going to be taken out of state and sold to a chemical company as lab animals for testing. The snakes and a couple of the other animals were to be sold to private collectors, but the bulk of the dogs, especially the bigger dogs, were headed to a dog-fighting ring based in Arkansas."

I was already feeling lightheaded at the thought of those bunnies and cats being used to test the effects of chemicals, but when he mentioned the bigger dogs being promised to the dog fighters, I got downright queasy. With the combination of the two sensations, I was thankful to be sitting down.

"We've been working all day with the authorities in the other states this guy gave us. In all, about ten people have been rounded up, with warrants out for three or four more. It turns out that both the outfit in Arkansas and the chemical company have been under investigation by various federal authorities for a while. Thanks to you, both have been shut down."

"Wow." Just call me Ivy the Wordsmith, master of all things . . . wordy.

Luke grinned, then reached over to pat me on the knee. "We couldn't have done any of this without the information you gave me. If you hadn't insisted on me checking it out on Tuesday, there's no telling how many of those animals would have been lost forever. You did a good thing, Ivy. Really good."

I could feel the heat creeping up my neck, and I hoped that being blinded by the light over my head kept Luke from seeing me blush.

"I'm just so glad we got them all back." My response sounded lame to my ears, but it was all I had. "I appreciate your help in this, Luke. I can't thank you enough for listening to me the other night and acting on it so quickly."

"Well, you were pretty insistent—and your buddy, Williamson, weighing in and pointing out that you'd probably go take care of it yourself didn't hurt things any." Swaim glanced over his shoulder in the direction of James' house. "Will you pass along our findings for me?"

"Absolutely," I said on an exhaled breath. I knew there was something else I should be saying, but for the life of me, I couldn't think of what it was. The fault for that rested squarely on the shoulders of the man across from me. He had on a dark blue shirt that made his eyes appear a deeper, more vibrant color than I'd ever seen before. And when he smiled, I could swear I saw a sparkle—an *actual* sparkle!—in those eyes. I stared for a moment, then blinked as the elusive thought finally settled in so I could give it voice. "I really appreciate you tossing the work over at PAWS in my direction."

"Aw, that was nothing. Besides, I wanted to try to help you win back a few of those customers who were so quick to ditch you . . . largely because of me."

"Some of them would have found a reason to drop me, regardless. That's just the nature of the beast. Thanks to the news coverage, several people have called me to reschedule, and I've picked up a few new clients, as well. That wouldn't have happened if you hadn't given me the opportunity to go out there and show people that I'm trusted. So, thank you."

"You're welcome." Luke dipped his head after he spoke, making me wonder if it was his turn to blush. "So, did Miss Anna came home today?"

"She did. I picked her up at lunch."

"Did I see you this morning, in town, picking up a

hitchhiker?"

An abrupt chuckle tumbled from my mouth. It was obvious, once again, that I couldn't get away with anything in Pinnacle.

"I was in town this morning, gassing up before I went to get Anna, but I didn't pick up a hitchhiker." The look on Swaim's face told me he was skeptical. "I gave a ride to an acquaintance, a guy I recently met who was just here for a little while. He was headed to Dallas, so I gave him a lift as far as I was going."

Luke nodded, still looking doubtful. "You might be a little too trusting, Ivy, but as long as you got back safely, that's all that matters."

I started to protest but ended up saying nothing. He was right, after all, so why should I argue?

"I know you have a little girl to tend to, so I'll get out of your hair," the detective stated as he got to his feet. When I moved to do the same, he extended a hand to help me, then seemed hesitant to let it go. We stood there in silence, looking at each other for more than a heartbeat or two. "Ms. Ivy, I'd like to take you out some evening. Maybe take you for a nice dinner and some dancing. Do you like to dance?"

His invitation was so sweet and sincere that I do believe I almost swooned.

"I used to love to go dancing, but I haven't done it in years," I answered honestly. "I'm not even sure I remember how."

"Aw, Ms. Ivy, dancing is like driving a car—once you learn, it's pretty hard to forget."

I chuckled and stepped away, removing my hand from his light touch. "Well, Luke, I'll give it some thought, but I think a couple of things are going to have to happen before I can go out with you."

"What would they be? Do I need to send you flowers or ask your father for permission?"

Swaim's smile told me he wasn't completely serious. At the same time, I was so charmed by his extremely old-fashioned suggestions that I forgot half of what I was going to say.

"First, you might have to stop calling me *Ms. Ivy*," I said.

"Why would I do that? Your name is Ivy, isn't it? Or should I call you Ms. IndigoViolet?"

I laughed. It seemed the detective was taking a page from my book on how to act obtuse.

"Only my mother calls me IndigoViolet. Just 'Ivy' is fine."

"Okay, then, *Ms. Ivy*," he said, emphasizing my name so that I knew he wouldn't change anything in that area. "What else do I need to do before you'll let me take you out on the town?"

I crossed my arms over my ribs, more to hold in a girlish giggle than to ward off the night's increasing chill. Based on some of the things he said, I was beginning to wonder if Luke had arrived in Pinnacle via time warp, as opposed to only relocating from New Orleans by way of an earthly vehicle.

"I think it might be wise if we hold off until you get a case where I'm not a suspect." My words and expression were serious now. "I don't want people to think I'm going out with you just to get away with something."

"Fair enough," he conceded, his face shifting into a genuine grin. Luke nodded and stepped off the porch. "I'll be sure to keep you updated on my caseload so you'll know when to signal the all-clear."

"That would be helpful, thank you," I spoke around a chuckle.

"Good night, Ms. Ivy," Luke said as he began to back away in the direction of his car.

I was beginning to wave to him when I remembered his other reason for visiting. "Luke, wait. What was it you needed to give me?"

"I can't believe I almost forgot!" He snapped his fingers and dug something out of his back pocket. When the detective stepped back into the light, he said, "I believe this belongs to you."

My mouth dropped open. In his hand was a formerly white but now brownish-red shoe. I know it was once white because its similarly stained mate was on the porch behind me. All I could do was laugh and take it from him.

"Someone with the crime scene technicians found it behind that little building where they were storing all those animals. I told them I didn't think it was pertinent to the case since it's too small for a grown man to wear."

"Uh . . . thank you," I managed to spit out.

"No problem." Luke winked at me as he again began to back away. "You have a nice night, Ms. Ivy."

I waited until he was in his car and had the motor going before I waved and went back inside, dropping the shoe he'd brought next to the one by the door. It was apparent that I'd have to dunk one in the mud more fully (and then put it through the wash) before I had a matching pair.

I was tired. It had been another eventful day in an all-around lively week, and I hadn't had anywhere near enough sleep. I paused at Anna's door before moving off to my own room, wanting nothing more than to gaze at the sleeping form of my baby to assure myself that she was truly home. From the light in the hallway, I saw that she was on her side, a smile on her face and her bottom inches from the edge of the bed. She was curled around an oddly shaped lump. I stepped closer, avoiding the creaky floorboards and making sure I didn't block the hall light. Between the slumbering form of my child and the black and white fur of Robin, lay Strawberry.

Part of me wanted to snatch the piglet up and deposit her outside with the chickens. Another part of me wanted to go find a camera to document the adorable sight that I internally swore would never occur again. In the end, I did neither of those things. I brushed Anna's hair from her face and placed a light kiss on her temple, then I patted Robin on the head and went off to find my own bed.

As I drifted off to sleep, I thought of people judging each other, and the last few words Anna and I had exchanged before I'd left her to answer the door. I could already imagine what direction our conversation would take in the morning.

Anna, why would you want to sleep with a squeaky, stinky little pig?

But Mama, my little girl would reply, *Didn't Jesus say we shouldn't judge?*

SUSAN BYRDE

Author Bio:

Susan Byrde is the author of the romantic
suspense series Abby's Road and the picture
book The World is Mine. After earning Masters
degrees in both Education and Business, Susan
has spent the last several years pursuing her
dream of becoming a published author. She uses
her experiences as a classroom teacher and other
professional positions to create realistic and
relatable characters in her newest series, The Ivy
Greene Mysteries. Susan is a member of the
American Christian Fiction Writers and has
served as a judge in several writing contests.
Susan makes her home in East Texas with her
husband, two rescue dogs, and a pair of small
parrots.

Social Media: Instagram- byrde8629

Facebook:
https://www.facebook.com/susanbyrde

Twitter: @susan_byrde

Website: susanbyrde.com

Made in the USA
Monee, IL
16 January 2021